SECOND CHANCES

NAVIGATING LOVE'S COMPLEXITIES

PK SRIVASTAVA

Dedicated to My Parents

Late Satyendra Prasad & Late Usha Srivastava

Contents

Disclaimer

This book is a work of fiction. Names, characters, places, and incidents are either the product of the author's imagination or used in a fictitious manner. Any resemblance to actual persons, living or dead, events, or locales is entirely coincidental.

Why This Title?

The title "Second Chances: Navigating Love's Complexities" is chosen with deep consideration, perfectly capturing the essence and overarching themes of the book. This title resonates with the universal appeal of second chances, a concept that embodies hope and the possibility of redemption and renewal during life's inevitable challenges. It speaks directly to our shared human experiences, reflecting the innate desire for growth and improvement, especially within the complexities of personal relationships.

The phrase "Second Chances" adds a significant layer to the title, suggesting the journey that characters undertake through the intricacies of love. Love, in its many forms-whether familial, platonic, or romantic-is rarely straightforward. The stories delve into how characters manage these multifaceted relationships, making choices and sometimes stumbling along the way, yet always moving toward a deeper understanding or reconciliation.

Furthermore, the title promises depth and relatability, setting an expectation for the reader that the book will explore rich emotional landscapes and the nuanced decisions that accompany human connections. It hints at a narrative journey that's not only about the characters and their stories but also offers reflections on how to navigate life's emotional challenges effectively.

By encapsulating themes of redemption, emotional navigation, and the universal quest for second chances within relationships, the title "Second Chances: Navigating Love's Complexities" effectively prepares the reader for a collection of stories that are both emotionally resonant and insightful, offering a mirror to our own lives and a map to traverse the often-convoluted paths of the heart.

Foreword

Life often provides us with unexpected detours, moments that demand reflection, courage, and the resolve to try again. "Second Chances: Navigating Love's Complexities" by PK Srivastava is a luminous exploration of these very moments.

It's a narrative woven with the universal threads of love, loss, redemption, and the quiet heroism required to rebuild what once seemed irretrievably lost. At its heart, this book delves into the deeply human yearning for renewal.

The title, "Second Chances: Navigating Love's Complexities," is not merely a nod to a theme but an invitation to embark on a journey through the lives of characters who are navigating the labyrinth of relationships and life-altering decisions.

Set against vibrant backdrops, from the bustling streets of Mumbai to serene college towns, the narratives explore the intricate interplay of ambition, emotions, and the quest for meaning. PK Srivastava's writing is a masterful blend of elegance and simplicity, making profound observations about the human condition accessible to every reader.

The stories traverse the terrain of emotions-from the quiet desperation of a mother striving to rebuild her life after an unthinkable loss to the bittersweet complexities of rekindled first loves.

Through every twist and turn, the characters face choices that test their limits and redefine their perspectives, offering us glimpses into our own lives and relationships. What sets this collection apart is its nuanced portrayal of second chances as more than just acts of grace-they are transformative journeys.

Whether it is through the catharsis of forgiveness, the courage to embrace vulnerability, or the resilience to rebuild shattered dreams, these stories resonate with an authenticity that lingers long after the last page is turned.

Critically, "Second Chances: Navigating Love's Complexities" achieves a delicate balance: it entertains while provoking introspection.

Each narrative is a mirror reflecting the triumphs and tribulations of human connections. Srivastava's prose is both evocative and restrained, leaving enough room for the reader's imagination to roam while delivering moments of poetic clarity that stay etched in memory.

Readers will encounter characters like Ayesha, whose strength in the face of profound personal tragedy becomes a beacon of hope; Rohan, who learns to reconcile duty and desire; and Marilyn, whose emotional growth offers a poignant lesson in self-discovery. These vignettes are not just stories-they are life lessons, gently urging us to examine our own decisions and the possibility of redemption.

This book is particularly relevant in an era marked by rapid changes and shifting relationships. It reminds us of the timeless truth that while we cannot undo the past, we can always rewrite our futures. As we navigate through the challenges of our modern lives, "Second Chances: Navigating Love's Complexities" offers solace and inspiration, urging us to believe in the power of love, resilience, and renewal.

It is with great admiration for PK Srivastava's ability to capture the essence of life's second acts that I recommend this book to you. Whether you are seeking inspiration, solace, or simply a beautifully told story, "Second Chances: Navigating Love's Complexities" will meet you where you are and perhaps, gently, guide you to where you need to be. So, turn the page and begin this journey.

Discover within these stories not just the trials and triumphs of their characters but reflections of your own capacity to endure, grow, and embrace the extraordinary potential of second chances.

Rajeev Bhadauria

I would like to extend my heartfelt gratitude to Mr. Rajeev Bhadauria for his mentorship and guidance provided to me. With an esteemed career spanning over nearly three decades, including pivotal roles, such as that, of Group President of HR

at Reliance ADAG, Global Group Director of HR at Jindal Steel and Power, and as a Senior Industry Expert for India and South Asia, at Mercer HR, Mr. Bhadauria has significantly influenced professional journeys of several people including their personal development. His insights and leadership have been instrumental in shaping my approach to strategic human resource management and leadership.

Currently, a Global Speaker, Mentor, and Executive Coach, as Managing Partner at Ebullient Consultancy, LLP, his contributions to the field of People management, continue to inspire and impact many professionals, including myself.

Prologue

Welcome to "Second Chances: Navigating Love's Complexities" a literary exploration that delves into the intricate dynamics of love, ambition, and the legacies we strive to create. This collection of stories opens a window into the lives of individuals who find themselves at life's crossroads, confronting the profound impacts of their choices and the unexpected twists of fate.

Set against a backdrop ranging from the rugged cliffs along Mumbai's shores to its vibrant city squares and serene suburban enclaves, each story is a vignette of life's complexities. Our characters face pivotal moments that challenge their perceptions and test their resolve. From high-stakes corporate battles and illicit romances to silent, introspective struggles within, the narratives reveal how extraordinary circumstances can emerge from the seemingly mundane.

At the heart of each tale is a quest for meaning and authenticity. Through their journeys, our characters encounter the full spectrum of human emotion-from betrayal and regret to hope and redemption. A couple seeks to reignite their once vibrant connection amidst layers of deceit; a young professional wrestles with the lingering pull of a bygone relationship as he tries to move forward; an entrepreneur watches the dual collapse of his personal and professional worlds, only to uncover his real calling in the ruins.

"Second Chances: Navigating Love's Complexities" does more than recount these stories-it invites the reader to engage deeply with them, to reflect on their own life experiences through the lens of the characters' trials and triumphs. This book serves as a reminder of the resilience of the human spirit and the power of love to redefine our lives, often surfacing in the least expected places and moments.

As these characters navigate their paths through loss and rebirth, their stories illuminate the enduring potential for growth and renewal. They teach us about the strength required to forgive and the courage needed to step into new beginnings, leaving behind a legacy of hope and transformed connections.

Let us turn the page and step into this journey, intricately penned not just to entertain, but to inspire-echoing the heartbeats of all who cherish the belief in the profound power of second chances.

Preface

Welcome to the intricate tapestry of human emotions that "Second Chances: Navigating Love's Complexities" unfolds. In this book, we traverse the intimate corridors of the heart, exploring the delicate interplay of life's trials and triumphs through stories that resonate with the universal quest for redemption and love.

Each narrative, while unique in setting and character, converges on the profound theme of second chances. This theme mirrors our inherent longing to overcome life's hurdles and heartaches. As you delve into the lives of Ananya, Rohan, Maya, and others, their stories offer both a reflection of our own experiences and a glimpse into the lives of others. Through these windows, you'll see the power of resilience, forgiveness, and hope in reshaping lives.

The creation of this book marked a personal journey of self-discovery and reaffirmed my belief in love's transformative power. It allowed me to delve deep into the complexities of relationships, exploring the fragile bonds that unite us and the unpredictable forces that can drive us apart. These tales capture moments of vulnerability and strength, despair and joy, betrayal and profound loyalty.

Follow Vijay and Meena, estranged yet linked by their past, as fate brings them together on a Mumbai's Metro Line 3 train ride. In the bustling backdrop of the city, their story reveals the quiet connections that redefine love and illuminate forgotten paths.

This collection also celebrates the quiet heroism in everyday lives, whether it's a single mother embracing new beginnings, a young professional facing the shadows of past romances, or an elderly couple rekindling their bond against the backdrop of youth's echoes. Each story honors the indomitable spirit of humans to heal and love again, even when hope seems lost.

Moreover, "Second Chances: Navigating Love's Complexities" invites you to reflect and perhaps see your own life mirrored in these stories. It's my hope that they inspire you to believe in new beginnings and recognize the extraordinary in the ordinary.

Thank you for choosing to explore these narratives. May they resonate with you and inspire reflection, just as they have inspired me to write them.

Step aboard and let the journey rekindle the embers of nostalgia.

Punit Srivastava

Acknowledgements

As I reflect on the journey that led to the creation of "Second Chances: Navigating Love's Complexities", I am overwhelmed with gratitude for the people who have shaped my life, guided my steps, and supported my dreams. This book is not just a product of my imagination, but a testament to the unwavering support and love I've received along the way.

Primarily, I wish to express my deepest gratitude to my beloved parents, Late Satyendra Prasad and Late Usha Srivastava. Your unconditional love, sacrifices, and teachings have been the foundation of my life. Your strength and wisdom continue to inspire me every day, and I dedicate this work to you. Though you are no longer physically present, your values, love, and guidance live on in everything I do.

To my extended family and dear kin, your constant encouragement has been a source of strength. You have been there through every milestone, every challenge, and every success. The bonds we share have given me the resilience to pursue my dreams, and for that, I am eternally grateful.

To my friends, both near and far, thank you for being my sounding boards, my cheerleaders, and my sources of laughter. Your belief in me, even when I doubted myself, has been invaluable. You have filled my life with joy, wisdom, and camaraderie, and I am so fortunate to have you all by my side.

A special mention to Rajeev Bhadauria Sir, Global Speaker, Mentor, and Executive Coach, and Managing Partner at Ebullient Consultancy, LLP. Rajeev Sir, your experience as Ex Group President HR at Reliance ADAG and Global Group Director HR at Jindal Steel and Power, combined with your tenure at Mercer HR as the Senior Industry Expert for India and South Asia, has profoundly influenced my professional path and personal growth. Your guidance across nearly three decades in these leading roles has been invaluable.

To my extended family, friends, and relatives, thank you for being a part of my journey. Your support, both seen and unseen, has provided me with a network of love and encouragement that I treasure deeply. Your presence has enriched my life in countless ways.

Lastly, to my better half, Shobhna, you have been my unwavering source of strength and understanding. Your belief in me, your patience, and your support through every endeavor have been my greatest blessings. I am forever grateful for your love, companionship, and the joy you bring into my life.

To our children, Aditya and Samriddhi, you both inspire me every day. Aditya, your intelligence, curiosity, and drive make me proud beyond words, while Samriddhi, your creativity, kindness, and vibrant spirit fill our home with joy. Together, the three of you make my world complete, and I am truly blessed to have such a wonderful family by my side.

This book is not just mine; it is the culmination of all the love, guidance, and support I've been blessed to receive throughout my life. To each of you who have been part of this journey, I offer my heartfelt thanks. Without you, this work would not have been possible.

Punit Srivastava (P.K.)

CHAPTER ONE

TRACKS OF NOSTALGIA

Vijay and Meena first met in the monsoon-soaked lanes of suburban Mumbai, where the rain was less an interruption and more a backdrop to the beginning of their teenage romance. Vijay, a lanky, bespectacled youth with an earnest smile, was drawn to Meena's vivacious spirit and her infectious laughter that echoed above the clatter of local trains. Their courtship blossomed swiftly amid shared college classes, stolen moments under shared umbrellas, and long walks along the Juhu beach, where the sunset seemed to paint their dreams in vibrant hues.

Their love, youthful and untested, stood defiant against the towering wall of familial disapproval. Vijay, a reserved and thoughtful soul from a modest railway family, and Meena, spirited and spontaneous, born into a lineage of affluence and tradition, had little in common by societal standards. Their bond, however, had grown quietly yet fiercely nurtured in fleeting glances, stolen conversations, and the hush of dusk when the world slowed down just enough for love to bloom in silence.

When reason failed to bridge the chasm between their families, the two made a bold choice-one that only the very young or the very brave could muster. Hand in hand, they climbed a small hill outside the city, away from the noise of judgment and expectation. At its summit stood an old temple, weathered by time, yet dignified in its solitude. It became their sanctuary.

There, under the fading orange canopy of a setting sun, they exchanged vows that held no grandeur, only truth. The priest, elderly and wise, sensed the sincerity in their eyes and did not ask too many questions. A few close friends stood as witnesses not to a rebellious act, but to a moment of quiet courage. Meena wore a simple saree borrowed from her friend, and Vijay's shirt was still creased from the morning's rush. There were no garlands, no elaborate rituals only the trembling sincerity of promises whispered into each other's ears, sealed not by spectacle, but by the weight of love untainted by expectation.

That hilltop temple far removed from their fractured world below became the symbolic peak of their love, where emotion triumphed over logic, and dreams momentarily outshone doubt. In that instant, they weren't just escaping they were choosing.

The years that followed their quiet hilltop wedding were a mosaic of moments some vibrant with joy, others dulled by hardship. Vijay poured his energy into his entrepreneurial ventures, often stretching himself thin to meet aspirations that once seemed just within reach. Meena, whose dreams of becoming a designer remained tucked away like a cherished sketchbook never opened, took up a teaching job to support the family, balancing lesson plans with lullabies. Together, they built a modest but warm home, eventually welcoming two children into their lives.

Their son, Rohit, with Meena's irrepressible laughter and boundless curiosity, brought sunshine into their days. Priya, quiet and observant like Vijay, became her father's silent confidante. For a while, the chaos of parenting stitched their days together, their love evolving from passion to partnership. But as the children grew more independent, the spaces between Meena and Vijay quietly widened. Conversations turned into logistics, and shared glances into silent dinners. Financial strains and the slow erosion of unspoken dreams weighed heavy on them. The spark that once burned fiercely on a hilltop began to flicker, dimmed by time and routine.

After more than two decades of shared history, they found themselves at a lawyer's desk signing papers with hands that once clutched each other in defiance of the world. It was a mutual, if sorrowful, understanding that what they once fought so hard to build had quietly unravelled. Theirs wasn't a story of regret, but of realism of love that was real, but not always enough to weather the passing years.

Now, after twenty years, fate or perhaps the gentle mischief of the universe seated them side by side in the bustling coach of the newly inaugurated Metro Line 3. It was a chance encounter, yet it felt as if time had been waiting for this very pause. The train halted unexpectedly between stations, and in that moment of stillness, Vijay and Meena turned toward each other, their eyes widening in shared surprise before softening into the kind of gaze only those with a shared past could hold. The narrow confines of the metro seemed to compress not just space, but time years melted away, unspoken words floated between them, and a familiar silence settled, one that once needed no translation.

Surrounded by strangers and the soft hum of delay-induced impatience, they sat quietly, their breaths syncing almost imperceptibly. There were no grand gestures, no dramatic confrontations only a quiet surrender to memory and meaning. In that suspended moment, the metro didn't just ferry passengers across a city; it bridged the distance of decades between two once-lovers now bound by a matured, bittersweet affection.

As the coach gently rocked forward again, Meena's softly-voiced question tentative, yet warm broke the silence like sunlight through morning mist. And suddenly, Vijay was transported. The present blurred, and he was once again a younger man, standing beside Meena on their first Diwali together. The memory unfurled like a well-preserved painting: fireworks exploding above, a sky alive with celebration, and Meena, glowing in a crimson sari that shimmered like the night itself. Her laughter, bright and unrestrained, had echoed over the rooftops, while Vijay clad in a cream kurta, his eyes fixed on her as if she were the only light he needed stood utterly enchanted.

In that fleeting moment on the metro, they weren't just remembering they were reconnecting, perhaps even healing. It wasn't about rekindling what was lost, but honouring what had been. And sometimes, that too, is love.

Meena, "Do you remember our first Diwali incident?"

Vijay paused, his eyes lighting up with the memory as if the sparklers from that night were mirrored in his gaze. "How could I forget?" he replied, his voice a mix of nostalgia and warmth. "You tried to light a rocket and it went sideways instead of up. I've never run that fast in my life!" He laughed, a genuine, hearty sound that

Meena hadn't heard in a long while.

Meena chuckled, her eyes crinkling at the corners. "And you still managed to be my hero that night dodging danger just in time," she said, her tone softening. The remembrance of their first Diwali together brought a spark back into their conversation, a reminder of their shared moments of joy and spontaneity.

Meena continued, "And when I had stolen your charm by the song I had sung and people went mad over it."

"Of course, I remember," Vijay replied, his voice tinged with nostalgia. "You stole the show that night, just as you've stolen this moment." His words, though simple, were laden with the weight of unspoken emotions, a tender acknowledgment of their shared past.

Meena's cheeks flushed with a rosy tint, much like the first blush of their early days of marriage when every glance had been a discovery, every touch a revelation. "You were quite the charmer, Vijay. Always knew how to make me feel like the only woman in the world," she reminisced, her hand reaching out to gently squeeze his.

Vijay chuckled, his eyes crinkling at the corners. "Was? I think I still might have a bit of charm left," he teased, his tone playful yet sincere. "Remember how we escaped the crowd that night, just to have a moment alone by the garden?"

Meena nodded, the memory flooding back. They had slipped away from the festive chaos, finding solace in the quiet garden lit only by the moon and the flickering diyas.

Vijay reached across the table, taking her hand in his. "I miss us, Meena," he admitted, his voice breaking slightly with emotion. "I miss how we used to be before life got so... complicated."

Meena squeezed his hand, her heart aching with the recognition of their mutual loneliness and longing. "I miss us too, Vijay. Maybe we got so caught up in where we thought we should be that we forgot to cherish where we are, and who we're with."

Vijay nodded, a look of resolve forming on his face. "Let's try to find our way back to each other," he proposed. "Not just for the sake of our past but for our present and future together."

Vijay had taken her hands in his, and in the soft glow, his eyes had spoken volumes. "It was our new beginning, but I wanted every moment to feel like it was just us," he had said.

"And now, here in this metro, it feels like it's just us again," Meena whispered, the closeness of the space wrapping around them like a cocoon. The chatter of the other passengers faded into a gentle hum, leaving only the resonance of their shared memories.

Their conversation, once shadowed by the weight of unresolved emotions and years of silence, gradually softened. The tension that had lingered in their voices began to melt, replaced by quiet laughter and shared memories. What started as hesitant small talk transformed into a gentle rediscovery of familiar quirks, of long-forgotten habits, of a connection that had merely been buried, not broken. In the ebb and flow of their words, the heaviness gave way to something lighter, something warmer a renewed understanding. It wasn't just nostalgia pulling them together; it was the realization that perhaps, even after all the years and distance, the path ahead might still have space for the two of them walking side by side once more.

Vijay reached over to tuck a stray strand of hair behind her ear, a familiar gesture that sent a shiver down Meena's spine. "It does, doesn't it?" he agreed, his voice low and husky. "If I could turn back time, I would find more moments like this, steal more escapes with you."

"Let's start with this Diwali," Meena suggested, a hopeful smile touching her lips. "Let's create new memories, just like that first time. Let's fill our home with light, laughter, and love again."

Vijay's agreement was immediate and enthusiastic, a shared resolve to rekindle the joy and closeness they once took for granted, starting with the festival of lights.

Years back, Vijay and Meena's arranged marriage was a grand spectacle, a true embodiment of North Indian nuptial traditions. Hosted in a lavish banquet hall adorned with marigolds and strings of jasmine, their wedding was a vibrant affair. Families and friends from distant towns gathered, their attires a riot of colours. Rituals were performed under a beautifully decorated mandap, where ancient chants filled the air, sealing their union.

The early days of their marriage were filled with discoveries and subtle surprises. Vijay, charmed by Meena's infectious laughter and culinary skills, often surprised her with evening walks by the riverside and small gifts that spoke volumes of his growing affection. Meena, appreciative of Vijay's thoughtful gestures and his unwavering commitment to their family, often wrote him little notes of love, hiding them in his workbag. Their romance blossomed amidst shared cups of chai and cozy monsoon evenings spent on the balcony, wrapped in shared blankets, watching the rain.

However, as the years wore on, the weight of unmet personal dreams began to cloud their shared joy. Vijay, a budding entrepreneur, found himself more at the office, chasing a vision only he could see. Meena, who had put aside her aspirations of studying design, felt a growing void as she navigated the quietude of their large, empty home. Conversations that were once filled with dreams and laughter gradually turned into discussions of schedules, bills, and responsibilities. The distance grew, not just in their conversations but in their hearts. Their home, once filled with shared dreams, slowly morphed into a silent battleground of individual ambitions, each unspoken, each growing heavier with time. The initial joy and shared dreams gradually gave way to a silent battleground of individual ambitions. The tapestry of their marriage, once vibrant and envied, now revealed the fraying edges of a union bound by tradition but strained by the pursuit of unfulfilled personal aspirations.

Vijay's business acumen was rooted in a profound understanding of the textile industry combined with an insatiable ambition to innovate and expand. He had a keen eye for identifying emerging markets and was adept at forging strategic partnerships that enhanced his family's brand on a global scale. His approach was analytical yet daring, often venturing into markets others deemed too risky. This ability to see potential where others saw peril paid dividends, allowing him to diversify the product lines and integrate cutting-edge technology into manufacturing and distribution processes.

However, Vijay's dedication to his business had significant personal costs. His relentless pursuit of success meant that his calendar was a jigsaw of international meetings, trade shows, and business negotiations. His physical presence at home became increasingly rare, and when he was home, his mind was often preoccupied with the next deal or the next trip. This gradual but growing distance began to strain his relationship with Meena, who found herself shouldering the emotional and domestic responsibilities alone. Despite understanding and initially supporting his ambitions, Meena struggled with the loneliness and disconnect that came from being a secondary priority to Vijay's expanding business empire. The physical distance between them grew into an emotional chasm, making it difficult to maintain the closeness they once cherished.

Meena, on the other hand, harboured a quiet longing to explore her artistic talents, a dream gently nurtured since her youth. Her passion for painting, which had been relegated to the background during the early years of marriage and motherhood, began to resurface with a force she could no longer ignore. Her canvases became her solace, filled with vibrant colours and bold strokes that reflected her deep-seated desire for independence and self-expression.

The tipping point came one fateful Diwali, years after their first. The festival, which had always been a time of togetherness for the couple, highlighted their growing disconnect. Vijay had planned a lavish party to court potential international investors, turning the intimate family gathering into a high-stakes networking event. Every detail was orchestrated, not for celebration but for impression.

Meena, feeling overshadowed and sidelined, decided to showcase some of her artwork at the party, seeking her husband's support to perhaps consider a gallery opening. However, amidst the flurry of business talks, her paintings went unnoticed by Vijay, who was preoccupied with sealing deals.

The night ended with a confrontation, both tired and frustrated. "Why can't you see that there is more to life than just expanding your empire?" Meena had pleaded, her voice a mix of disappointment and desperation.

Vijay, feeling attacked and misunderstood, retorted sharply, "And why can't you understand that everything I do is to secure our future, to ensure we maintain the lifestyle you enjoy?"

The argument that marked the beginning of the end was not explosive, but unravelling layer by painful layer. Long-buried frustrations and quiet disappointments surfaced, revealing how far they had drifted from the promises once whispered at a hilltop temple. The warmth that had once made even struggles feel bearable had cooled, replaced by silence that spoke louder than words. It became achingly clear that their shared journey, though meaningful, was no longer nurturing who they had become.

In the weeks that followed, their home was filled with quiet conversations, tearful pauses, and lingering glances that hinted at what was being lost. After many sleepless nights and difficult reflections, they arrived at the decision to part not with bitterness, but with a deep, unspoken gratitude for the years they had weathered together. Their passions, once the glue between them, had grown into dreams too different to coexist under the same roof.

Yet, in choosing to let go, they honoured what they had built preserving the dignity of their love rather than letting it wither in resentment. Their goodbye was not a collapse but a careful folding away of a shared chapter one that would always remain etched in memory, tender and irreplaceable.

Their children, now leading independent lives in the UK, had long been the common thread that kept Vijay and Meena loosely connected a shared responsibility that gently nudged them toward civility, even as life pulled them in different directions. Festive video calls, milestone updates, and coordinated visits had kept the channels open, though often just enough to maintain appearances.

But today, within the stillness of a halted metro coach, those roles momentarily faded. They were no longer defined by their titles as parents or ex-partners. Stripped of obligations and expectations, they were simply Vijay and Meena once again two people with a rich past, a quiet understanding, and a trove of memories tucked away in the corners of their hearts. In that suspended moment, they found comfort not in closure, but in companionship rediscovering the ease of old friendship, one shared smile at a time.

The train eventually lurched forward, resuming its journey through the city's veins, but something about that suspended moment lingered a pause not just in motion, but in time. In the quiet between stations, amidst the hum of a world rushing by, their young love stirred once more. It wasn't the fiery passion of youth, but a softer, steadier glow an ember long buried beneath the ashes of life's trials, now gently reignited.

Their conversation, once cautious, now flowed with ease peppered with laughter, reflective silences, and glances that said more than words ever could. In those stolen moments, Vijay and Meena weren't just revisiting the past; they were discovering how much of it still lived within them. The memories weren't heavy anymore they were warm. And as they sat side by side, two seasoned hearts tempered by time, the thought quietly emerged: perhaps, in the twilight of their lives, there was room yet for a tender new beginning a second chapter written not in haste, but in understanding.

When the train finally reached the next station, they stepped off together no longer burdened by the weight of what had been, but buoyed by the unexpected comfort of reunion. Their steps were lighter, their hearts quietly fuller.

They had boarded as two distant figures connected only by memory, but alighted as something more companions rediscovering the quiet magic of familiarity. What had once been lost to time and circumstance now shimmered with the possibility of renewal not in the same form, but in something gentler, more grounded.

In the months that followed, what began as an accidental encounter evolved into a comforting rhythm. Their meetings became a quiet routine unhurried lunches at cafés that still held echoes of their past, long walks where silence felt natural, and laughter rose without effort. Together, they retraced the contours of their shared story, revisiting old haunts not as former lovers, but as old friends slowly stitching together the frayed edges of their bond.

These moments, shaded by nostalgia but brightened by newfound clarity, brought with them not only forgiveness but a deeper understanding of themselves, of each other, and of the enduring thread that had weathered time, distance, and change. In those simple acts of reconnection, a new chapter quietly began one not rooted in expectation, but in the quiet joy of presence.

As winter slowly surrendered to the soft bloom of spring, something within them, too, began to blossom. What had started as tentative conversations on a delayed metro ride grew into a gentle rhythm of companionship unforced, familiar, and slowly deepening. The comfort of old memories gave way to the excitement of new ones, and in each other's quiet presence, they rediscovered not only laughter but also a sense of belonging they hadn't felt in years.

This time, they spoke of the future not with the guarded caution of the past, but with the quiet joy of those who had known loss and found something precious again. There was no rush, no pressure just a shared understanding that life had offered them a rare second chance. Long walks turned into weekend plans; shared meals turned into shared dreams.

By the time Diwali arrived a season once etched in memory with the golden glow of their early love they had made a decision. They would reunite their lives, not as an attempt to recreate the past, but to honour the bond that had survived it. This time, their union was born not from youthful urgency, but from seasoned affection and mutual respect. It was a conscious choice one rooted in resilience, in forgiveness, and in the quiet certainty that what they now shared was both new and enduring.

That Diwali, as diyas flickered once again across balconies and courtyards, their hearts glowed with something familiar yet renewed. The festival that had once marked the height of their early love now became a symbol of a love reawakened not bound by the expectations of marriage or the weight of old roles, but shaped by companionship, warmth, and the beautiful possibility of what still lay ahead.

As Vijay and Meena slowly rebuilt the delicate fabric of their relationship, the ripple effects reached their families first as gentle murmurs of curiosity, then as waves of cautious hope. Initially, there was hesitation, even quiet concern. The scars of their past separation weren't easily forgotten, and those closest to them feared the possibility of reopening old wounds. But as days turned into weeks, and weeks into a steady rhythm of togetherness, something began to shift.

What once felt uncertain began to feel reassuring. The air around family gatherings grew noticeably lighter. Conversations that had long been measured and guarded slowly transformed into open-hearted exchanges. The subtle spark between Vijay and Meena the shared smiles, the soft teasing, the ease of their old companionship was no longer hidden. It was visible, and more importantly, it was sincere. Their children, Rohit and Priya, who had once been the bridge between them, became silent witnesses to this transformation. They observed their parents not with skepticism, but with a quiet respect for the courage it took to mend what had frayed.

Small affirmations emerged in unexpected ways. Vijay's aging father, a man of few words and many judgments, began offering nods of approval during conversations, his sternness giving way to a gentle pride. Priya noticed it in the way he lingered during family dinners, choosing to stay a little longer at the table, listening, smiling. Meena's mother, once wary of her daughter's emotional well-being, now spoke of her with light in her voice and hope in her words. Her once-concerned gaze softened into one of peace as she watched Meena laugh freely again.

Even the extended family the uncles and aunts who had once exchanged hushed whispers of doubt began to acknowledge the quiet strength in what was unfolding. No longer were they asking, "Will it last?" but instead saying, "It takes great strength to love again." Their tone had changed from caution to admiration. They spoke openly now of the resilience it takes to rebuild, and the grace required to forgive not just each other, but themselves.

What emerged wasn't just acceptance, but a collective embrace. A recognition that this wasn't merely a rekindling of a romance, but a reclaiming of a bond built through both joy and hardship. And in those subtle gestures in the warmth of a shared meal, the support of a knowing glance, the return of laughter around the dinner table Vijay and Meena found something even deeper than reunion: they found belonging, not just with each other, but within the hearts of those who mattered most.

The Festival of Lights, Diwali, arrived with its familiar sparkle, but this year, it carried a deeper meaning one that transcended the glow of lamps and the rhythm of firecrackers. This time, the Diwali celebrations carried a quiet depth one that extended beyond the glittering lights and joyous rituals. Surrounded by family, laughter, and the warmth of acceptance, Vijay and Meena found themselves not looking back in regret, but forward with hope. And so, under a sky ablaze with fireworks and hearts alight with possibility, Vijay and Meena stood hand in hand not as a couple restarting from where they had left off, but as two souls who had found their way back, wiser, softer, and deeply grateful. Their journey had come full circle, not by retracing old steps, but by choosing new ones together.

Their home, once echoing only with memories, now brimmed with renewed laughter, gentle chatter, and the comforting sounds of family reunited. Diyas flickered in every corner, as if lighting not just the rooms, but the unspoken corners of their hearts. The scent of sweets, the vibrant rangolis, the soft melodies of festive songs all felt more meaningful this time, not just as tradition, but as quiet witnesses to something tender and rare: a love rediscovered. This Diwali, the lights didn't just dispel the darkness outside it illuminated the paths of those brave enough to walk back to each other, not to relive the past, but to reimagine the future. It reminded everyone present that life, with all its turns, always offers second chances not just to mend what was broken, but to build something even stronger.

This time, the celebrations were more profound, emphasizing that life does indeed offer second chances not merely to correct the past but to create a future that is even better, anchored in mutual support, understanding, and renewed dreams.

CHAPTER TWO

Whispers of a Faded Dreams

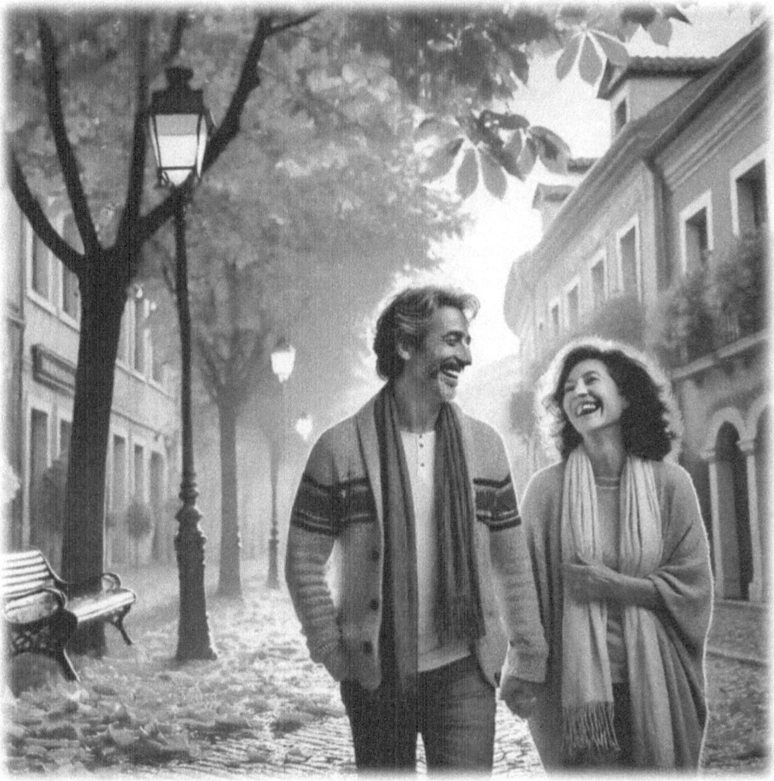

Ananya Mehta, the only daughter of the late business magnate Vivian Mehta, found solace and peace among the verdant hills of Dehradun, far removed from the relentless pulse of Mumbai, the city that had defined her family's legacy. As a student at Doon College, she immersed herself in her academics with a fervor that was partly driven by a desire to forge her own path, one distinct from the towering shadow of her father's empire.

The tranquil environment of Dehradun provided a stark contrast to the vibrant chaos of Mumbai, where her life had once been a whirlwind of social engagements and lofty expectations. Here, in the quietude of her college town, Ananya often wandered through the misty mornings, reflecting on her mother, Ayesha's tales of a young and vivacious love with Rohan Rai, a charming entrepreneur whose life had once intertwined deeply with hers in the bustling city.

Those stories, filled with passion and youthful dreams, resonated with Ananya, stirring a longing for a connection that transcended the complexities of her family's wealth and influence. She longed to experience the kind of love that had once set her mother's world ablaze-a love that was pure and exhilarating. Amid the calmness of her new surroundings, Ananya's heart ached slightly for the thrilling chaos of Mumbai, yet she appreciated the serene moments of introspection that Dehradun afforded her, as she continued to carve out her own identity, one thoughtful step at a time.

Years ago, in a coeducational school in Mumbai, Rohan and Ayesha were classmates and sweethearts, their young love budding in the corridors and spilling over the monsoon-soaked streets.

Ayesha and Rohan's romance was the kind that left behind notes in school lockers and hearts doodled in the margins of notebooks-sweet, innocent, and deeply unforgettable. It began over shared textbooks and little glances that lingered a second too long during chemistry class. There was a certain magic in their silences, a quiet thrill in brushing hands while reaching for the same pencil.

Rohan was the first to confess, one rainy afternoon beneath the old banyan tree outside their school-a place that had quietly witnessed the blooming of countless teenage dreams. Nervously, he pulled out a crumpled piece of paper, the ink slightly smudged from his clammy hands. It was a poem-raw, clumsy, but brimming with sincerity. Ayesha read it, smiled through the drizzle, and whispered yes, her cheeks flushed like the pages of a romance novel come to life.

From that moment on, their world became one of whispered phone calls after curfew, shared earbuds playing their favorite love songs, and long walks home just for the excuse of being near each other a little longer. At the local ice cream parlor-their sacred weekend spot-they laughed over melting scoops of chocolate and strawberry, their fingers playfully sticky, their gazes soft and unguarded. Each giggle, each playful nudge, felt like a new vow whispered beneath the chaos of adolescence.

In those fleeting years of teenage wonder, they weren't just a couple. They were each other's universe-young hearts writing their first story of love, with wide-eyed hope and dreams that stretched as far as forever.

As the golden hues of the setting sun spilled across the horizon, Ayesha and Rohan pedaled side by side, their bicycles weaving through the winding village paths like whispers of a fleeting dream. Laughter rang out between them, light and carefree, carried on the breeze like a secret song only they knew. The world around them became a blur of color-emerald fields, amber skies, and the soft blush of twilight melting into the earth.

Their hands brushed now and then, sending sparks through their fingertips, hearts beating in rhythm with the turning wheels. With every breathless pedal, they raced not just against the wind, but the inevitability of goodbye. And yet, in that golden hour, nothing else mattered. Time stood still-just a girl, a boy, and the kind of love that makes even the fading light feel eternal.

But as all perfect days do, this one too slipped quietly into dusk, the golden warmth of their shared world slowly giving way to the chill of impending separation. Rohan's departure loomed like a shadow neither of them could ignore, turning each glance, each touch, into something sacred.

The train station buzzed with movement, but for Ayesha and Rohan, time seemed to slow. The air was thick with the scent of steel and smoke, the screech of brakes and the low murmur of announcements a distant hum compared to the pounding of their hearts. Their fingers intertwined desperately, as if holding on tightly enough could freeze the moment.

Rohan brushed a tear from Ayesha's cheek with a trembling hand. "We'll meet again," he whispered, his voice catching. "Someday. Somehow."

With tears glistening in her eyes, Ayesha nodded, her voice barely audible. "No matter how far, I'll wait."

They sealed their promise with a kiss that was soft, trembling, and filled with all the words they couldn't say. It was the kiss of first love saying goodbye-heartbreaking in its purity, unforgettable in its tenderness.

The final whistle sliced through the air like fate calling time. As the train pulled away, Rohan leaned out, his eyes locked on hers until distance claimed him. Ayesha stood motionless on the platform, her heart full and aching, the echo of his goodbye lingering like the last notes of a beautiful song.

It wasn't just an ending. It was a pause-etched in memory, wrapped in hope-waiting for destiny to turn the page.

Rohan's father, bound by the duties of his career as a railway officer, received an unexpected transfer to Pune, pulling at the seams of the tightly woven bond between Rohan and Ayesha. As Rohan prepared to leave, his heart was laden with promises he had whispered and those he had left unspoken, each one a silent pledge to return to her. Ayesha, on the other hand, was left to navigate the bustling streets of Mumbai alone, her presence at college marked more by her absence of spirit than her physical attendance.

Rohan's departure had struck Ayesha like a sudden storm, leaving her world drenched in a sorrow that was profound and penetrating. Each day, as she sat in the lecture halls, her mind wandered to the memories of their laughter echoing through the corridors of her heart, their dreams that had mingled like the monsoon skies of their city. The future they had envisioned together seemed to crumble piece by piece, leaving her to gather the fragments in silent despair.

Her efforts to concentrate on her studies were constantly thwarted by the ache in her heart, a relentless reminder of her loss. The once vibrant and ambitious Ayesha now found herself grappling with a loneliness that was as overwhelming as the city's monsoon seas. With Rohan gone, the colours of Mumbai seemed duller, and the sounds of the city, once a symphony of dreams, now tolled like a bell of her solitude.

College life ushered Ayesha into the bustling, eclectic social whirl of Mumbai, a stark contrast to the quaint simplicity of her hometown. Here, amidst the glittering skyline and the relentless pace, she was introduced to Vivian Mehta-dashing, innovative, and the epitome of urban sophistication. Vivian, known for his groundbreaking ventures and magnetic presence, seemed to personify the city's unyielding ambition and vibrant pulse.

With Vivian, every encounter was an adventure, an unexpected delight that swept Ayesha into a whirlwind of exhilaration. Their midnight drives were magical, the cool sea breeze mingling with the salty tang of the coast as they sped along the Marine Drive, the city lights reflecting like scattered jewels on the water's surface. These moments, under the vast, star-lit sky, seemed to stretch time, holding the promise of infinite possibilities.

Vivian's penchant for surprise dates added layers of excitement to their budding romance. He had a way of peeling back the layers of Mumbai, revealing its hidden gems-rooftop cafes with panoramic views, secluded beaches bathed in moonlight, and vibrant bazaars that buzzed with life until the early hours. For Ayesha, each date was a revelation, the city unfurling before her like a vibrant tapestry of sights, sounds, and smells.

As their relationship deepened, the pain of Ayesha's past-her heartfelt goodbye to Rohan at the train station-slowly receded into the corners of her heart. It was not forgotten, but rather transformed, into a bittersweet chapter of her youth. With Vivian, her heart began to mend, filling anew with hope and joy. The memory of Rohan lingered like an old song, poignant and sweet, but increasingly overshadowed by her present-a vibrant dance of light and shadows, love and laughter, with Vivian by her side.

On that serene evening, as the sun dipped below the horizon, painting the sky in mesmerizing shades of orange and purple, Vivian Mehta steered his yacht into the calm waters of the Arabian Sea. The city's skyline, a distant silhouette against the twilight, twinkled like a constellation laid upon the earth. Ayesha stood beside him, her hair gently tousled by the sea breeze, her eyes reflecting the fiery hues of the sunset.

As the yacht bobbed gently on the waves, Vivian turned to Ayesha, his eyes alight with a mixture of anticipation and adoration. The world seemed to hold its breath, the only sounds the soft lapping of the waves against the hull and the distant hum of the bustling city.

"Isn't it beautiful?" he asked, gesturing towards the horizon where the sky met the sea in a perfect line.

"It's breathtaking," Ayesha replied, her voice a soft whisper, carried away by the wind.

Vivian took her hands in his, their warmth mingling as the cool air enveloped them. "Ayesha, these past months with you have been the most incredible journey of my life. Every moment with you is a discovery, a new reason to fall deeper in love."

Ayesha's heart fluttered, her pulse quickening as she looked into Vivian's earnest eyes. "Vivian, I..."

He smiled, squeezing her hands gently. "I brought you here because I couldn't imagine a more perfect place to ask you this. Ayesha, will you marry me? Will you be the one I wake up to every day, the one I dream with, the one I grow old with?"

Tears welled up in Ayesha's eyes, joy and love overwhelming her. "Yes, Vivian," she breathed out, her voice trembling with emotion. "Yes, I will marry you."

Vivian slipped a delicate ring onto her finger, the diamond catching the last rays of the sunset, sparkling like the sea around them. They embraced, the city lights and the starry sky above them bearing witness to their promise-a promise of a future filled with love, stability, and endless adventures.

As they stood there, the ocean vast around them and the city bustling behind, they felt a profound sense of togetherness, a perfect harmony between their souls and the infinite universe around them. This moment, simple yet profoundly romantic, was a testament to their love-a love that had grown quietly but passionately, ready to stand the test of time.

Ayesha and Vivian's wedding was the epitome of splendor and grandeur, capturing the vibrant essence of Mumbai's elite. The venue was breathtaking, nestled in one of the city's most luxurious locales, with the Arabian Sea providing a majestic backdrop that sparkled under the moonlit sky. The air was electric, filled with the allure of Bollywood celebrities mingling with business moguls and societal luminaries, all brought together by the union of two young hearts.

The entrance to the celebration was draped in cascades of lush, fragrant flowers, from delicate jasmine to vibrant marigolds, setting a path that led to a world of wonder. Inside, the venue was transformed into a dreamlike setting, with thousands of fairy lights woven into the decor, creating a canopy of stars that twinkled above the gathered guests.

At the heart of it all were Ayesha and Vivian, who stood hand in hand under an ornate archway adorned with roses and peonies, their petals soft and perfumed, adding a touch of romantic serenity to the opulence around them. The ceremony was a beautiful blend of tradition and contemporary elegance, reflecting the couple's personalities and their shared vision of life together.

As they exchanged vows, their voices steady but filled with emotion, there was a palpable sense of magic in the air. The vows were not just words; they were heartfelt promises, weaving their dreams, hopes, and futures together. The moment their hands tied the sacred thread, the crowd erupted in applause, a joyous acknowledgment of the union not just of two individuals but of two powerful families.

The reception that followed was nothing short of spectacular. Live music from renowned musicians filled the air with melodies that ranged from classical rags to contemporary hits, ensuring the dance floor was never empty. The array of cuisines offered was a gastronomic delight, featuring dishes from around the globe, each prepared to perfection, embodying the couple's shared love for adventure and fine dining.

As the night drew on, the celebration continued, with laughter and music echoing under the starry sky. Fireworks lit up the horizon, their colors bursting in sync with the beats of music, mirroring the explosive happiness of the newlyweds and their guests. It was a night of uninhibited celebration, a fitting start to Ayesha and Vivian's journey together, marked by love, ambition, and the promise of a future as limitless as the sky under which they had vowed to walk together.

In the blissful chapters that followed, Ayesha embraced her new life of luxury with grace. The arrival of their daughter, Ananya, was celebrated with joyous fervour, marking a new beginning in their journey. Ananya grew up enveloped in love and the warmth of her parents' profound bond, her laughter a sweet melody in their lives, echoing through the halls of their grand home. Her birth not only symbolized the continuation of their legacy but also infused a new spectrum of love and happiness into their lives.

The arrival of their daughter, Ananya, had transformed Vivian and Ayesha's lives in the most tender, profound way. Her first cry had woven a new kind of music into their world-a rhythm that pulsed with joy, discovery, and a love that defied explanation. From the moment she wrapped her tiny fingers around theirs, their hearts had found a new center.

Their home, once filled with soft jazz, books, and quiet dinners, now bloomed with lullabies, colorful toys scattered across the floor, and the melodic laughter of a child discovering the world. Toddler Ananya brought with her a whirlwind of firsts-wobbly steps on the garden grass, delighted squeals as she chased bubbles under the afternoon sun, and babbling conversations that made no sense but brought endless smiles.

"Mama, look!" she would cry out, wide-eyed and pointing at a butterfly fluttering near the marigolds. Her world was one of wonder, and in witnessing it, Ayesha and Vivian found theirs anew.

Ayesha would lift her gently, press a kiss to her soft curls, and whisper, "Yes, my love, it's beautiful-just like you."

Vivian, ever the storyteller, would join their little adventures with childlike enthusiasm. He built castles out of cushions, turned mealtime into picnics under blanket forts, and spun bedtime tales where unicorns befriended monsters and little girls saved enchanted forests. He delighted in her giggles, her curiosity, and the way she called him "Papa" with such earnest affection.

As Ananya grew, her tiny hands learned to draw hearts and flowers with crayons, her feet tapped to music she made up on the spot, and her eyes sparkled with questions about the moon, the stars, and where butterflies go at night. Her presence stitched every corner of their home with a golden thread of love-finger paintings on the fridge, lullabies hummed in harmony, and sleepy cuddles that ended every long day.

Each evening, after the stories and the songs, after kisses were placed on cheeks and stuffed animals tucked in beside her, Ananya would murmur through half-closed eyes, "Goodnight, Papa. Goodnight, Mama." And as her breathing slowed, the house would fall into a silence not of emptiness, but of peace.

In her, Ayesha and Vivian had found a love reborn-a soft, growing flame that lit up their days and warmed their nights.

But the fabric of their perfect world began to unravel one fateful evening. Ayesha received a call that turned her very soul ice-cold.

Vivian had been in a car accident, they said, and it was serious. The floor seemed to slip away beneath her as she clutched the phone tighter, her other hand automatically reaching out to steady herself against the wall.

At the hospital, the harsh, sterile lights seemed to flicker in rhythm with her sinking heart. As they explained the situation, the doctors' words blurred into a distant echo. Vivian was gone, taken by a cruel twist of fate, leaving behind a void that was suffocating and immense.

Back home, Ayesha sat in Ananya's room, watching her daughter sleep peacefully, unaware of the storm that had just torn through their lives. Tears streamed silently down Ayesha's cheeks as she stroked Ananya's hair, whispering, "Papa loves you, my darling. He will always be with us, in every butterfly, every star."

The days that followed were a blur of condolences and hushed voices, the once vibrant memories now sharp fragments of a shattered dream. Ayesha found herself replaying the tender moments they had shared-Vivian's laughter filling their home, his eyes sparkling with mischief as he played with Ananya, their quiet conversations after their daughter had drifted to sleep.

In those moments, Ayesha would hold Ananya close, breathing in her scent, finding a fragment of solace in her presence. "We'll look after each other, won't we?" she'd ask, to which Ananya, with her innocent understanding, would nod and wrap her tiny arms around her mother.

The house, now too large and echoing with the ghosts of their past joy, became both a sanctuary and a prison of memories. Yet, through the pain, Ayesha knew she must rebuild, for Ananya, and for Vivian, whose love and dreams had woven the very fabric of their existence. As she faced each day, the weight of her loss was both a burden and a call to love stronger, to hold tighter to the little girl who was her last connection to the man they had so tragically lost.

As Ayesha faced the world alone, her every step was shadowed by the weight of her loss. The once lively gatherings and vibrant parties of Mumbai's elite now echoed with the silence of Vivian's absence. She transformed, almost imperceptibly, from the vivacious woman she once was into a pillar of strength, her resolve forged in the furnace of her pain. Widowhood draped its somber cloak around her shoulders, and she embraced single motherhood with a fierce determination, her love for Ananya becoming both a balm for her aching heart and a beacon guiding her through the fog of her grief.

Nostalgia often swept through her, a poignant reminder of her lost love, as she watched Ananya grow-each milestone a bitter-sweet slice of joy, each achievement a reminder of Vivian's absence. Ayesha's life was now a complex mosaic of past joys and present sorrows, each day a step in the long journey of healing and resilience, held together by the enduring love for her daughter and the memories of a past embroidered with the deepest affection.

Rohan's journey to becoming a decorated Major in the Army began with his resolute determination to clear the National Defence Academy (NDA) exam. His days were consumed by rigorous preparation, as he poured over books and honed his physical fitness. Each push-up and page turned fuelled his drive to serve his country. When the results came in, his name stood proudly among the successful candidates, a testament to his dedication and discipline.

At the Indian Military Academy (IMA) in Dehradun, Rohan's life transitioned into a regimented schedule marked by early mornings, challenging training sessions, and the forging of unbreakable bonds with his fellow cadets. The sprawling campus of the academy, nestled amidst the lush greenery of the Doon Valley, became his new home, where the crisp mountain air filled his lungs as he tackled obstacle courses, strategy classes, and leadership drills. The discipline was stringent, the expectations high, yet Rohan thrived, his resolve steeling with every challenge.

Despite the demands of military life, Rohan often found himself lost in nostalgia. The same hills that cradled the IMA also cradled memories of Ayesha, whose presence in Dehradun as a student overlapped with the geographical backdrop of his current life. The bittersweet memories of their shared dreams and tender moments in Mumbai lingered in his heart, untouched and vivid. Rohan kept these memories locked away, a precious trove that he revisited in his lonelier moments under the starlit Dehradun skies. His heart, though hardened by the rigor of army life, remained tender in its solitary remembrance of Ayesha. Now, stationed so close to where Ananya studied, the past seemed to echo around him, a constant reminder of what could have been-a life markedly different from the disciplined solitude he had embraced as a soldier.

On a gentle spring day, as the mild breeze carried the fresh bloom of Dehradun's abundant flora, Ayesha arrived to visit Ananya, her presence in the quaint town an echo of fate's subtle orchestrations. The universe, with its mysterious whimsy, steered her steps to a local book café, a cozy haven nestled among the whispering pines and bustling streets, where nostalgia mingled with the rich aroma of freshly brewed coffee.

The cafe, with its walls lined with shelves brimming with books and the soft hum of quiet conversations, was a sanctuary for those who sought refuge in the written word and the comfort of a warm cup. It was here, amid the rustic charm of worn wood and the soft glow of hanging lights, that fate decided to weave its old threads anew.

As Ayesha entered, the chime of the doorbell stirred Rohan from his thoughts. He had frequented this café during his rare off-duty hours, finding solace in the literature that reminded him of a life once dreamed of. Lifting his eyes from the pages of a novel, he found himself face to face with Ayesha, whose presence suddenly filled the room with a familiar warmth that he had long consigned to the corners of his heart.

Their eyes met, a torrent of unspoken memories flashing between them. The world seemed to slow, the chatter around them fading into a soft murmur, as they took in the sight of one another. Ayesha's smile, hesitant at first, blossomed as the initial shock gave way to a tender recognition. Rohan, equally moved, stood up, his military posture softening as he approached her.

Rohan, his voice tinged with a quiet intensity, broke the silence. "Ayesha... I didn't think I'd see you here. How have you been?"

Ayesha, her heart fluttering with a mix of surprise and old affection, replied softly, "Rohan, it's been years... I'm well, just visiting Ananya at college. And you? I see life has treated you well." She gestured to his uniform, a symbol of his commitment and sacrifice.

"Yes, the army has been my life. But it's nothing compared to the surprises life throws at you in a book café," he said with a slight chuckle, his eyes crinkling with a familiar warmth.

Their conversation flowed effortlessly as if no time had passed, yet with the weight of years behind each word. "Do you still read poetry, Rohan?" Ayesha asked, glancing towards the book in his hand.

Rohan smiled, "I do. It's one of the few things that hasn't changed. What about you? Do you still enjoy those mystery novels?"

"Yes, although these days I seem to find enough mystery in real life trying to keep up with Ananya," she laughed, her eyes lighting up with the mention of her daughter.

In the quaint book café, where the shelves were lined with stories of every hue, Rohan and Ayesha found themselves seated across from each other. The aroma of freshly brewed coffee mingled with the musty, comforting scent of old books. It had been years since they last met, and yet, as they spoke, it felt as if the intervening years had folded into mere moments.

Rohan reached across the table, his fingers brushing against hers as he passed her a cup of coffee. "I can't believe this," he murmured, his voice a blend of wonder and nostalgia. "After all these years, here we are."

Ayesha clasped the warm cup, her eyes meeting his with a softness that spoke of long-held affection. "Life has its ways, doesn't it? Leading us back," she replied, her voice low, reverberating with emotions long buried.

The sun outside dipped lower, casting streams of golden light through the café's windows, wrapping them in a cocoon of amber warmth. The light played across Rohan's face, highlighting the lines that time had etched since their parting. Ayesha noticed these subtle changes, each one a marker of the years they had spent apart, each a story in itself.

"Do you remember our last day together?" Rohan asked, leaning in slightly, his gaze locked with hers.

"How could I forget?" Ayesha smiled, a bittersweet edge to her words. "That day at the train station... It feels like a lifetime ago."

Rohan nodded, his smile tinged with regret. "I always regretted that it ended the way it did, without a proper goodbye."

"The goodbye we never really wanted," Ayesha added softly. The room seemed to shrink, the sounds of other patrons and the clink of coffee cups fading into the background.

Rohan took a deep breath, his eyes never leaving hers. "I've thought about you over the years, Ayesha. I wondered if you ever found what you were looking for."

Ayesha's hand trembled slightly as she set down her cup. "I did, and more," she paused, the weight of her next words hanging between them. "But I lost so much along the way."

The confession seemed to draw them closer, a bridge formed by shared understanding and mutual losses. Rohan reached out, his hand covering hers, a gesture filled with the familiarity of old love. "And yet here we are," he whispered, "sharing this moment."

Ayesha nodded, squeezing his hand. "Here we are," she echoed, her heart filling with a mixture of joy and sorrow. "Maybe that's all we need right now."

As the café continued to buzz quietly around them, their conversation drifted from past memories to their lives now—tales of travels, triumphs, and tribulations. In this corner of the world, where the scent of coffee and nostalgia was thick in the air, they rediscovered a piece of their past, a reminder of first loves and youthful promises, cherished now in the stillness of a golden afternoon.

They spoke of everything and nothing, their conversation a gentle stream flowing over rocks of past pains and present realities. Rohan met Ananya, who reminded him so much of Ayesha in her younger days. The connection was instantaneous, a bond forged anew on the anvil of shared histories. As they rekindled their friendship, the potential for something deeper, something enduring, seemed possible.

Now, with the past resurfacing through Rohan, Ayesha found her heart warring between the echoes of what once was and the stark realities of what could never be again. Their reconnection, though filled with the warmth of familiar affection, was also a reminder of the paths they had walked separately, the lives they had lived apart. Their coffee date is filled with laughter and reminiscences of the past.

Rohan: (with a chuckle) "Remember our old monsoon escapades? I still have a scar from when you dared me to jump over that giant puddle."

Ayesha: (laughing) "It was hardly a puddle, Rohan. You turned it into an Olympic event!"

Rohan: "Well, you always did inspire my more... athletic pursuits."

They share a warm, reminiscent laugh.

Ayesha: "Speaking of pursuits, I've been chased by Ananya's toddler-speed social calendar these days. If you think the military is regimented, try preschool birthday parties."

Rohan: "Sounds like a fierce battleground!"

Ayesha shares more about her daughter and her life as a mother, while Rohan talks about his career and the places it has taken him. The conversation naturally flows, and they find themselves closing the café, reluctant to end the night.

In the gentle embrace of the book café, surrounded by the soft hum of life and the scent of old pages and fresh coffee, Rohan and Ayesha found themselves at a crossroads carved by fate and filled with the echoes of what could have been. Their conversation, a tapestry woven with threads of nostalgia and new hopes, had bridged the gap of years and heartaches, reigniting a spark that neither had forgotten. Rohan walks Ayesha to her car, and in the dim light of the parking lot, they share a hesitant but tender kiss. They part with a promise to see each other again soon.

As autumn painted the town in hues of orange and gold, their meetings grew from tentative coffees to long walks under the fiery canopy of the trees.

During one of their long walks under the fiery autumn canopy:

Ayesha: "Can you believe we used to think staying up until midnight was rebellious?"

Rohan: (grinning) "Now, if I'm up that late, it's only because I've fallen asleep on the couch with the TV on."

Ayesha: "Oh, the wild nights of youth, replaced by the wild nights of... finding the best pillow support."

Rohan: "Hey, a good pillow is worth its weight in gold in my book." They both chuckle, enjoying the comfort of shared mundane truths.

With each step, each shared memory and laughter, the bond that had once seemed severed by life's cruel twists was mended, stronger, and more profound. Ananya, with the wisdom sometimes found in the young, saw the change in her mother, the lightness in her steps, the return of her laughter. She found in Rohan a friend, a confidante, someone who brought stories from the world outside and a glimpse into the mother's past, vibrant and alive.

The day Rohan proposed to Ayesha wasn't marked by grand gestures but by intimacy and the quiet comfort of certainty. In their favorite corner of the book café, amidst the whispers of countless authors and the silent witnesses of many a confession, Rohan knelt on one knee, his voice steady and his eyes holding Ayesha's.

Rohan: (kneeling) "Ayesha, will you make me the happiest man by turning my quiet evenings into blissful chaos with you?"

Ayesha: (teary-eyed, joking) "Only if you promise to help me decipher Ananya's teen lingo. I'll need all the help I can get!"

Rohan: "It's a deal, as long as you're the one dealing with any future math homework."

Ayesha laughs softly, nodding in agreement as she extends her hand.

The ring, simple yet elegant, was a symbol not just of a promise, but of a journey- of roads taken and roads yet to be explored.

The wedding, held as winter first touched the earth with its frost, blended old and new. It was witnessed by those who had seen their first chapter and those who supported their second. The celebration was heartfelt, and the joy was palpable and as pure as the first snow.

Life, in its quiet and relentless rhythm, marched on. Rohan and Ayesha found themselves slowly rediscovering the tenderness they had once put away-sharing coffee and conversation, gentle silences, and glances that spoke of healing and hope. Yet, just as their hearts began to open again, a storm arrived, swift and unannounced.

During a classified mission along the volatile northern border, Rohan was appointed to oversee a strategic operation involving intelligence sharing with a foreign ally. The mission, though successful on the ground, took an unexpected turn when leaked documents pointed toward a serious breach in protocol-one that occurred under his command. Though Rohan hadn't sanctioned the leak, his signature was on a file that had been tampered with, implicating him in a situation that questioned not just his leadership, but his integrity.

The military tribunal loomed ahead, and with it came media whispers, political agendas, and the agonizing possibility of suspension. For the first time in his service, Rohan felt shackled by a mistake he hadn't made-but one that nonetheless bore his name.

In the dead of night, seated on the bench outside his quarters under a sky burdened with clouds, Rohan called Ayesha. His voice trembled, the usually composed officer reduced to a man staring into the possibility of disgrace.

"I signed that file in good faith, Ayesha. I didn't know what they'd tucked into it. But it doesn't matter now. In their eyes, I'm responsible."

Ayesha's voice, when it came, was calm, firm-a whisper of strength wrapped in grace. "Rohan, you once told me the uniform doesn't just represent valor. It represents dharma-duty born of purpose. You did your duty with honesty. That is your karma."

Rohan sighed. "And yet, this karma might end my career."

"Then let it," she said gently. "Let it, if that's the price of truth. But don't become the man who hides behind silence to save his pride. That isn't who you are."

There was silence between them, until Ayesha continued, her voice now tinged with the clarity of lived experience.

"You know, when Vivian was alive, his business dealings often brought results—but not always with righteousness. I watched him win in the world but lose his peace. You have the chance to do both—to stand for what's right, not for what's easy. This is your dharma, Rohan. And I will stand by you, no matter how long or difficult that path is."

Her words hit him deeper than any court judgment ever could.

In that moment, Rohan realized this wasn't just about a file, a tribunal, or even his career. It was about the choice between moral courage and silent compromise. Between clearing his name with integrity or walking away from the storm with shadows trailing behind him.

Guided by Ayesha's clarity and the ancient wisdom she invoked, he made his decision. He would face the inquiry, defend the truth, and hold those responsible accountable-not with vengeance, but with dignity. His karma was to act, not to control the outcome. His dharma was to uphold what was right, even if it meant standing alone.

The process was grueling. Questions pierced like bullets, and suspicions clouded the air around him. But Rohan's calm resolve, backed by truth and transparent testimony, slowly dismantled the fog of doubt. Evidence surfaced. The truth emerged. And though not everyone applauded his stand, those who mattered understood the weight he bore-and the strength it took to carry it.

As the tribunal concluded, exonerating him of direct fault, Rohan walked out not with a sense of triumph, but of quiet peace. He had chosen the harder path. And he had done so not for glory, but for what his soul could live with.

In the days that followed, as he and Ayesha sat beneath the twilight sky with Ananya nearby, Rohan looked at them both and felt something he hadn't in years-a sense of true alignment. Between heart and duty. Between love and purpose. Between karma and dharma.

He had whispered once that some dreams fade with time. But now he knew-some dreams are only waiting for the right kind of courage to awaken them again.

Meanwhile, Ananya blossomed under the quiet strength of her mother and the steady presence of Rohan, who had gently evolved from a guardian figure into someone she deeply respected and trusted. Their home, once filled with echoes of loss, now pulsed with laughter, late-night movie marathons, and spirited debates over everything from global politics to the perfect pasta recipe.

College applications, which once loomed like a mountain of pressure, slowly transformed into an exciting journey-one they navigated as a team. Evenings were spent reviewing essays, shortlisting universities, and envisioning the future. The dinner table became a hub of animated discussions, filled with possibilities and dreams. Ayesha would offer her calming wisdom, Rohan his strategic thinking, and Ananya her curiosity and ambition. There were disagreements, jokes, and even moments of nostalgia-but above all, there was togetherness.

In this shared rhythm, Ananya found not just support, but inspiration. She saw in her mother resilience, and in Rohan, integrity-and in both, a love that had weathered storms and chosen healing. With their guidance, her world felt limitless.

Years later, as they sat in that same café, the scene almost unchanged except for the lines time had gently added to their faces, Rohan and Ayesha held hands under the table. Their daughter, now grown and as spirited as Ayesha had once been, chatted animatedly about her dreams, her plans, her future-her voice a beautiful echo of her mother's.

Amidst the clink of coffee cups and the rustle of turning pages, Ayesha leaned closer to Rohan, her eyes shimmering with the soft glow of remembrance.

"Do you remember," she began, her voice tinged with nostalgia, "those endless summer evenings we spent walking along the shoreline, how the sunset would paint the sky just as we reached the old lighthouse?"

Rohan smiled, the corners of his eyes crinkling as he nodded, "How could I forget? You used to say the horizon was where our dreams lay waiting for us. It seems like a lifetime ago, yet I can still feel the sand beneath my feet when I think of those days."

Ayesha chuckled, her laughter mingling with the warm air of the café. "And the time you tried to impress me by climbing to the highest rock, only to get stuck waiting for the tide to recede. I think that was the moment I realized how much I loved your adventurous spirit-even when it got you into a bit of trouble."

Rohan's laughter joined hers, a rich sound that filled the small space. "I was quite the hero, wasn't I? Stranded atop my rocky throne, hoping my damsel would save me with more than just a teasing smile."

Their shared laughter faded into a comfortable silence, filled with the unspoken acknowledgment of the precious memories they had woven together, a rich tapestry of youth and love revisited in the quiet corners of the café they had once called their own.

Outside, the world continued its hurried pace, but inside the café, time stood still- capturing forever the beauty of a second chance fully realized.

CHAPTER THREE

CATCHING DREAMS

35

Yuvraj Patil grew up in a modest neighborhood in Pune, where the lively streets harmonized with the ambitions of its inhabitants. The son of a dedicated schoolteacher and a nurturing homemaker, Patil's childhood was humble yet enriched with the warmth of supportive parents. His father, recognizing the spark of innate cricketing talent in Yuvraj, nurtured his son's fervor for the sport. From a young age, Patil was captivated by cricket, his passion fueled by watching the game's legends perform heroic feats on a flickering television screen at home. Despite the family's limited finances, his father wholeheartedly supported his cricketing aspirations. By taking on extra tutoring jobs, he managed to gather enough to buy Patil his first cricket kit, setting the stage for a journey driven by determination and a deep love for the sport.

Yuvraj Patil's journey from the narrow lanes of Pune to the broader cricketing landscape was built on countless hours of dedication and the unwavering support of his family. From the moment he received his first cricket kit-a gift born of his father's sacrifices-Patil immersed himself in the sport with unrelenting zeal. His early mornings were spent perfecting strokes against the compound wall, and evenings echoed with the thud of leather on willow at local practice nets. Over the years, his raw talent began to take shape under the watchful eyes of seasoned coaches who recognized not just his skill, but his hunger to grow.

It was during a crucial club match that Yuvraj's cricketing journey took a significant leap forward. The local ground, bathed in golden sunlight, buzzed with excitement as aspiring cricketers and loyal fans gathered in anticipation. Clad in his club's colors, Yuvraj stepped onto the pitch with a quiet resolve that had become his trademark. Facing a renowned fast bowler whose pace had rattled many before him, Patil remained unflinching. His poise under pressure and laser-sharp focus stood out, and as the first few deliveries came in, he began crafting a masterclass.

His batting that day was a symphony of technique and intuition. Every boundary he struck seemed deliberate, as though guided by an inner rhythm honed over years of disciplined practice. His footwork was crisp, his timing impeccable-glorious cover drives, flicks off the pads, and a couple of towering sixes punctuated his innings. But Yuvraj wasn't just a batsman. When it came time to field, he moved with the agility of a seasoned athlete, saving crucial runs and energizing his teammates.

It was this all-round brilliance that turned heads-not just among the spectators, but also in the stands where state selectors had come scouting for emerging talent. What they witnessed was more than just a good innings; it was a statement. Yuvraj Patil had arrived, and he was ready for the next big leap.

This match marked a defining turning point in Yuvraj Patil's cricketing journey. His ability to remain composed under pressure, paired with an impressive display of skill across both batting and fielding, underscored his readiness for the next level of competition. He didn't just perform-he commanded attention. The poise with which he handled the game's challenges, the flair in his strokeplay, and his athletic presence on the field all painted the portrait of a cricketer destined for greater arenas.

For the spectators, it was more than just an entertaining match-it felt like the unveiling of a future star. Every stroke Yuvraj played carried the weight of a dream long nurtured in silence and sacrifice. Coaches exchanged knowing glances, selectors scribbled notes with newfound urgency, and young cricketers on the sidelines watched in awe, whispering his name with the reverence reserved for legends in the making. That afternoon, something shifted-not just for Yuvraj Patil, but for everyone who bore witness to the spectacle of his talent.

This wasn't merely a personal triumph; it was a collective realization. The boy from Pune, who once played with borrowed bats and taped tennis balls in cramped bylanes, had finally stepped into the limelight. Backed by the unwavering support of his father-who had believed in his son's potential long before applause had entered the picture-and strengthened by the discipline honed through years of quiet perseverance, Yuvraj's journey was finally taking flight.

The match turned out to be more than just a milestone; it was the gateway to a new world. A formal call-up to the state team followed within weeks, and Yuvraj seized the opportunity with the same fierce determination that had guided him since childhood. Match after match, he turned heads with his consistent performances-gritty innings under pressure, agile fielding, and an innate ability to read the game like a seasoned pro.

Soon, the whispers became headlines. His name began to circulate in cricketing circles, and it wasn't long before the blue jersey-the very symbol of his boyhood dreams-was within reach. When the day finally arrived and he was selected to represent India, it felt like destiny affirming what those close to him had always known: Yuvraj Patil wasn't just talented-he was meant for greatness.

His debut on the international stage was electric. The same calm composure that once held steady under club-level pressure now shone under the scrutiny of global audiences. His bat spoke eloquently, silencing critics and winning over fans. With every confident pull shot and impeccably timed cover drive, Yuvraj carved a place for himself in the hearts of millions.

He wasn't just playing cricket-he was performing poetry in motion. Commentators praised his technical brilliance, teammates admired his quiet leadership, and the nation embraced him as one of its own. From television ads to magazine covers, Yuvraj Patil became a household name, a symbol of what grit, grounding, and a relentless spirit could achieve.

But even amidst the rising fame, he never forgot his roots-the humble grounds of Pune, the weathered hands of his father, and the girl with dreams in her eyes who cheered louder than anyone else. Yuvraj Patil had become a star, but it was the memories of where he came from-and who stood beside him-that gave his journey its true shine.

During his school years, Patil met Maya Singh, a fellow student who shared his love for sports, though her passion was in filmmaking. Their friendship quickly blossomed into a sweet, high school romance. During one such outing of Yuvraj and Maya at a local fair, Maya said (teasingly) "I bet you can't win me one of those giant teddy bears!"

Yuvraj: (with a grin) "Prepare to be amazed, then. I plan to win you two, so you remember this day twice as much!"

Maya: (laughing) "Greedy for memories, are we?"

Yuvraj: "Only the best ones with you."

Maya was a constant presence at every match Yuvraj Patil played, easily recognizable as the most enthusiastic and vocal supporter in the stands. Her cheers, filled with unfiltered joy and unwavering belief, cut through the noise and always found their way to Yuvraj's ears. For him, her presence wasn't just comforting- it was grounding, a reminder of who he was and why he played.

As time passed, their friendship evolved beyond shared laughs and schoolyard memories. They became each other's confidants, celebrating small victories and supporting one another through quiet setbacks. What began as a childhood bond gradually matured into something deeper and more intimate-a love rooted in understanding, shared dreams, and a connection that went far beyond the boundaries of the cricket field.

Their romantic encounters often unfolded under the soft, quiet skies after Yuvraj's matches, when the crowd had dispersed and the floodlights dimmed, leaving behind a gentle hush over the field. The scent of fresh grass lingered in the air as they walked slowly along the boundary ropes, their fingers sometimes brushing, sometimes intertwining, in a silent symphony of closeness. The world around them faded, and it was just the two of them-young, hopeful, and deeply connected.

Their conversations were never just casual-they were intimate glimpses into the hearts of two dreamers. Yuvraj would explain the subtleties of cricketing strategies, the mental dance between bowler and batsman, the thrill of a perfectly timed shot. In return, Maya opened up about building layered characters and weaving emotions into a compelling screenplay. They spoke in different languages-sport and cinema-but the emotions were the same: passion, purpose, and a desire to leave a mark.

These late-night exchanges became the soul of their relationship. The ease with which they confided in one another, the way Maya's laughter lingered in Yuvraj's mind like the melody of a favorite song, and the warmth in his eyes when she spoke of her dreams-it all deepened their bond in ways neither fully understood but both deeply felt. Their love wasn't dramatic or rushed; it was tender, evolving naturally like the slow bloom of a night flower, nourished by trust, admiration, and a promise that they would chase their dreams-hand in hand.

As they navigated the tumultuous waters of adolescence, their relationship became a quiet refuge-a steady anchor in a world that often felt uncertain. In whispered conversations under starlit skies and lingering glances exchanged across crowded school corridors, they built a dreamscape of their future. Yuvraj envisioned roaring stadiums, the tricolor on his chest, while Maya saw herself behind the camera, weaving stories that touched hearts.

Their dreams, though different in form, beat with the same rhythm-one of passion, purpose, and unwavering belief in each other. What bound them wasn't just youthful affection but a deeper love, rooted in shared ambition and nurtured by gentle encouragement. Their vision for tomorrow sparkled with the promise of success, not in solitude, but in the warmth of each other's arms-growing together, dreaming together, rising together.

When Yuvraj Patil was selected to play for the national cricket team, it marked a monumental step toward realizing the dreams that he and Maya had cherished together. The news brought waves of jubilation to his family, who had watched his ascent from local fields to national arenas with a mixture of pride and awe. For Maya, Yuvraj's selection was not just a testament to his cricketing prowess but also a reflection of his relentless determination and the spirit of a man ready to embrace the global stage.

Together, they celebrated this achievement, acknowledging it as a pivotal moment in their journey. Maya, always his staunchest supporter, saw this as the beginning of a new chapter where Yuvraj could showcase his talent on an international scale, while she continued to pursue her ambition in filmmaking, inspired by his success to chase her own dreams with equal fervor. Their shared vision for the future seemed more tangible than ever, bound by achievements that were both personal and shared, driving them forward hand in hand.

By now, Yuvraj had proudly worn the Indian cricket team jersey, the iconic blue clinging to his frame like a second skin, heavy with pride and purpose. As they strolled along the quiet boundary lines after a match, he would speak of his experiences on the international stage-of roaring crowds, high-stakes games, and the indescribable feeling of representing the nation. His eyes would light up with the same boyish spark that once spoke of dreams, now transformed into stories that made Maya smile with quiet pride. She'd listen intently, often resting her head on his shoulder, before sharing her own dreams-vivid stories she longed to tell through her films, tales of strength, love, and hope inspired by the world as she saw it.

The trajectory of Yuvraj Patil's life took a devastating turn on a chilly November morning-a moment that cleaved his world into a clear before and after. What began as an ordinary drive through the misty roads of Lonavala quickly descended into horror. Near a quiet stretch by the local police station, Yuvraj's car lost control, veered sharply, and collided violently with a concrete road divider. In an instant, the vehicle was engulfed in flames, its bright orange glow piercing the early dawn like a cruel omen.

Inside that inferno, dreams were scorched beyond recognition. Maya-his soulmate, his fiercest supporter, the girl whose voice had once echoed through stadiums-was gone in a heartbeat. The fire took her before help could arrive, before a goodbye could be whispered, before a final glance could be exchanged.

Yuvraj, battered and burned, survived-but not whole. Trapped between consciousness and agony, he was pulled from the wreckage by rescuers unaware that the true damage lay not just in broken bones or torn ligaments, but in a shattered spirit. As news of the accident spread, the world mourned the rising filmmaker who never got to tell her stories. But for Yuvraj, it was more than a tragic headline-it was the obliteration of a shared future, a silencing of laughter, and the abrupt erasure of every plan they had painted together under the stars.

In that single, horrific moment, the vibrant colors of his life drained into grey. The cricket field, once his sanctuary, felt like a hollow ground. The cheers that once fueled him now rang hollow in memory. Maya was no longer there-in the stands, in the crowd, in his world. And Yuvraj, though alive, was left to carry a grief so heavy it threatened to crush everything he had ever stood for.

Severely injured, Yuvraj was quickly transported to a private hospital in Lonavala, known for its specialized treatment facilities. As he lay recovering from physical injuries, the emotional and psychological toll was immense. The dreams they had built together-of cricket stadiums filled with cheers and film premieres lit by camera flashes-suddenly seemed distant and unattainable. Yuvraj was left to grapple with the reality of continuing his journey without Maya by his side, a journey now overshadowed by grief and the echoes of a shared future that would never come to pass.

Yuvraj speaking to a therapist: (voice cracking) "Everything went dark, not just at night but even during the day. I feel like I'm stuck in a shadow that isn't passing."

Therapist: "It's okay to feel lost, Yuvraj. It's part of grieving. Maya meant the world to you."

Yuvraj: "She was my world. And now? It's like I'm learning to breathe with no air."

The Senior Superintendent of Police, Lonavala, Mr. Vikramjit Malik informed New India Times that Yuvraj was driving a BMW car which tragically hit the divider and caught fire. The unfortunate event occurred around the early hour of 3.30 AM.

The first thought that struck Yuvraj Patil immediately after the life-threatening car crash on 15th November 2022, was a profound and heart-wrenching loss. "First time in my life I felt like letting everything go. I thought my time in this world was finished," Patil described in a tearful interview with National Sports Network, titled Believe: To Death and Back, conducted in Chennai on August 12th, 2023, roughly ten months after the harrowing accident. "At the time of the accident, I was painfully aware of my wounds, but the loss of Maya, a wonderful person and my once beloved, was the greatest pain I had ever felt."

Their romance had been a series of unforgettable moments-quiet walks under the starlit skies, sharing dreams over long drives, and the soft whispers of future promises. They had laughed together at silly jokes and comforted each other during tough times, creating a tapestry of memories that now haunted Patil in the silence of his recovery room with his dad on his side.

Father: (holding Yuvraj's hand) "You have been through the worst, son. It's okay to cry, to feel the pain. But remember, you are not alone."

Yuvraj: (tears in his eyes) "I keep wondering, why her? Why us?"

Father: "Some questions in life remain unanswered, Yuvraj. But how we face them-that defines us."

Following the initial treatment in Lonavala, Yuvraj Patil was airlifted to Mumbai, where he faced one of the toughest battles of his life-not on the cricket field, but within the sterile walls of a hospital room. Multiple surgeries were performed to reconstruct all three ligaments in his right knee, the same leg that had once danced across the pitch, anchoring a nation's hopes. But the physical pain paled in comparison to the ache in his chest-the echo of Maya's laughter, the flash of her eyes during their rain-soaked dances, the unspoken dreams they had once woven together.

His world had grown quiet. The cheers of the crowd had faded into silence, replaced by the slow rhythm of IV drips and whispered footsteps in hospital corridors. Days blended into nights in a haze of medication and memories-until, one afternoon, the door to his room opened to a presence both unexpected and strangely comforting.

Jaan Kapur-the acclaimed Bollywood actress, known for her magnetic screen presence and a heart as luminous as her smile-stood hesitantly at the threshold. Clad in simplicity that contrasted her usual red-carpet glamour, she carried not the aura of a celebrity, but the quiet empathy of someone who understood pain.

She had followed Yuvraj's journey for years, not just as a fan of the sport but as someone genuinely moved by the grace and grit he brought to the game. News of his accident had shaken her. It wasn't just the loss of a brilliant cricketer, but the suffering of a soul she had silently admired from afar. Compelled by something she couldn't quite name, she reached out-not through public gestures or media soundbites, but through a personal visit, hoping to bring a sliver of comfort to someone whose resilience had once inspired her.

Their first meeting was laced with quiet tension and curiosity. Yuvraj, though surprised, welcomed her with the humility that had always set him apart from his fame. He had seen her on screens, but here she was in front of him-real, warm, and far more human than the silver screen allowed. Jaan, on the other hand, found herself unexpectedly moved by the vulnerability in his eyesthe kind of silent sorrow that didn't ask for pity, only presence.

What was meant to be a brief visit turned into a habit. Jaan found herself returning-first out of concern, then out of genuine connection. Her presence brought color to Yuvraj's monochrome days. She would walk in with fresh flowers or books, sometimes with anecdotes from her film sets, other times with no words at all-just the comfort of her company.

Their conversations flowed effortlessly, weaving through shared interests and unspoken emotions. Cricket and cinema-their respective worlds-became the common ground on which they began to build something new. From strategies on the field to stories behind the camera, from memories of personal loss to glimpses of guarded hope, they discovered not only a soothing companionship but a kinship born of resilience.

These meetings, filled with conversations ranging from cinema to cricket, forged a new friendship grounded in shared passions and newfound support.

As Yuvraj Patil and Jaan Kapur's friendship deepened, their conversations gradually moved beyond the familiar comfort of cricket and cinema. They became more intimate, more reflective-marked by pauses that spoke volumes and silences that didn't need filling. In Jaan, Yuvraj found not just a friend, but a quiet sanctuary, someone who didn't rush his healing but walked beside him through it.

Yuvraj began opening up about Maya-not just as a memory, but as someone whose presence still lingered in every corner of his heart. He spoke of the way she used to cheer for him, her voice always the loudest in the stadium; of the way she'd light up when they slow-danced in the rain; of the nights they stayed up planning futures that would now never come. He remembered the scent of her favorite perfume, the softness of her handwritten notes tucked into his cricket bag before every match, and the way she looked at him-not as a cricketer, but as a man she believed in more than he believed in himself.

His grief wasn't loud-it lived in the quiet moments, in the way he sometimes paused mid-sentence or looked away when the memories rushed in too quickly. Maya had been his compass, his calm in chaos, and her absence had left an ache no surgery could heal.

Jaan listened without interruption, her eyes often glistening with emotion. She never tried to replace Maya in his story-instead, she honored her. With a compassionate heart, she gently encouraged Yuvraj to treasure those memories, not as chains to his sorrow, but as stepping stones toward healing. Slowly, in the warmth of her understanding, Yuvraj began to rediscover fragments of peace-pieces of himself that he thought he had lost forever.

Jaan's visits soon became the highlights of Yuvraj's long days spent in rehabilitation. She brought with her an infectious laughter and a vibrancy that brightened the hospital's somber atmosphere. Her presence acted as a healing balm to Yuvraj's broken spirit. During one particularly poignant visit, as they shared a quiet moment looking out at the cityscape from his hospital window, Jaan gently took his hand, whispering words of hope and encouragement. It was then that Yuvraj realized he was beginning to smile again, not from obligation but genuinely, sparked by Jaan's unwavering support and kindness.

Their connection, rooted in shared tragedy and resilience, blossomed into something more profound, a tender bond that promised healing and perhaps, in time, a new love. This evolving relationship was marked by heartfelt discussions about future aspirations, where laughter and dreams began weaving into the fabric of their daily interactions, suggesting the possibility of new beginnings for both.

As Yuvraj Patil's rehabilitation progressed in Mumbai, his life began to take on a new rhythm, one marked by gradual healing and burgeoning hope. Jaan Kapur, who had initially stepped into his life offering solace in his darkest times, had become his constant companion, filling his days with light and laughter. Their friendship had deepened into a love that neither had expected but both had come to cherish deeply.

Yuvraj and Jaan on their first informal date had been to Marriott Hotel and chose the cozy corner table for privacy.

Jaan: (smiling) "So, cricket star, aside from bowling maidens over on the field, what's your secret talent?"

Yuvraj: (playfully) "I make a mean mango smoothie. It's the secret to my energy."

Jaan: "Is that an invitation to taste it, or are you just teasing?"

Yuvraj: "Consider it a promise to charm your taste buds!"

Jaan's influence on Patil was transformative. She introduced him to the world of cinema beyond the cameras, sparking in him an appreciation for storytelling that paralleled his own life's narrative.

Jaan speaking to Yuvraj during his recovery: "I read somewhere that broken things, when put back together, can be even more beautiful. That's you, Yuvraj. You're finding your pieces, but you'll shine again."

Yuvraj: "I never thought I'd find someone who understood my cracks."

Jaan: "We all have them; it's what makes the light get in."

Together, they attended film premieres and charity events, where Patil found a new platform to share his journey, contributing insights from his experiences to discussions on overcoming adversity and the importance of mental health in sports.

The public was captivated by their love story, drawing parallels between their cinematic romance and the tales Jaan portrayed on screen. Media outlets frequently covered their outings, and fans celebrated their resilience and mutual support. Patil, who had once captained his national team with stoicism, now spoke openly about the strength he drew from Jaan's presence in his life.

As Patil's physical strength returned, so did his prowess on the cricket field.

Coach: "It's good to have your back, Yuvraj. The team hasn't been the same without your spirit."

Yuvraj: "It took everything I had to come back. I'm not just playing for me anymore-I'm playing for Maya, for those who believed I could stand again."

Coach: "And that's why you're a true captain, on and off the field. Let's show them what you're made of!"

Yuvraj Patil marked a significant return to international cricket, achieving a century in his comeback match, a testament to his skill and perseverance. The overwhelming cheers from the stadium for Yuvraj weren't just for his performance but also for his journey of overcoming challenges, hinting at past hardships he's faced, such as injuries or personal struggles. Jaan's presence in the stands underscores her unwavering support. Her pride and emotional connection to Yuvraj's success add a personal layer to this professional milestone, showcasing the deep bonds that enhance and o On the same cricket field where Patil had celebrated his triumphant return, his personal life took a center stage as he planned a surprise proposal for Jaan. After a casual stroll around the pitch-supposedly to relive his century moment-Patil suddenly veered off script. Pretending to fumble for a lost cricket ball, he instead pulled out a ring, prompting a playful eye roll from Jaan, who teased him about his "fielding skills." His proposal was heartfelt and genuine, reflecting their shared simplicity and deep connection. Jaan, overwhelmed by his sincerity and the surprise, accepted with tears of joy, while a smattering of spectators who had stayed behind erupted into spontaneous applause, delighting in their happiness and turning the field into a scene straight out of a romantic comedy.

Patil and Jaan's wedding was a grand affair that perfectly married tradition with contemporary glamour, embodying the essence of both their worlds. Set against the stunning backdrop of Mumbai's luxurious skyline, the venue was adorned with intricate floral arrangements and elegant, modern decor that sparkled under crystal chandeliers. Traditional elements were woven throughout the event, with Patil in a regal sherwani richly embroidered in gold, while Jaan dazzled in a designer lehenga that shimmered with every step she took, reflecting her glamorous lifestyle.

The guest list was a who's who of celebrities, blending cricket legends with Bollywood stars, creating a spectacle that was constantly under the flash of paparazzi cameras. The ceremony itself was a beautiful mix of old and new, featuring classical rituals followed by a contemporary reception. An extravagant banquet hall hosted the event, where gourmet cuisine from around the world was served, alongside street food stalls mimicking the Mumbai chaat flavors for a touch of local zest.

As the evening progressed, the atmosphere buzzed with live performances from famous musicians and heartfelt speeches that echoed through the venue, celebrating both Patil and Jaan's achievements and their journey together. The night culminated in a spectacular fireworks display over the bay, symbolizing the bright future awaiting the couple. The wedding wasn't just a union of two people but a festive gathering that celebrated their enduring love and the blending of their distinct yet harmonious lives.

Post-marriage, Patil and Jaan founded a charity focused on providing sports and arts education to underprivileged children. This endeavour combined their passions and allowed them to give back to the community that had supported them through their respective careers. They travelled together, worked on projects that fuelled their creative and altruistic passions, and continued to inspire those around them with their dedication to making a difference.

As years passed, Yuvraj Patil and Jaan Kapur became symbols of hope and love's power to transcend all adversities. Their story, filled with unexpected turns, deep loss, and profound love, was often cited as a real-life tale of finding love when least expected and rising together against all odds.

As Yuvraj Patil settled into the twilight years of his life, he often mused on the concept of second chances. His life had been a testament to this phenomenon-rising from a horrific tragedy to find not just professional redemption but deep personal fulfilment alongside Jaan. Their life together, marked by mutual support and profound affection, demonstrated how second chances could foster unexpected growth and joy.

During a public speaking event, Patil shared his reflections on second chances, addressing an audience captivated by his journey. "Life," he began, his voice imbued with the weight of experience, "throws at us challenges we think we cannot overcome. I lost a part of my soul (Maya) in that crash, a loss I believed was the end of my story. But life had other plans, plans that included a second chance at love, a new dawn with Jaan, who became my strength."

He continued, "Our story could have been one of loss, but together, we chose to make it one of hope, of building bridges from the pieces of our broken dreams. We found love in each other, a love that was unexpected but all the more precious because it was a second chance."

Yuvraj's message resonated deeply, not just with those who had faced personal tragedies but also with those seeking to redirect their paths in life. His and Jaan's efforts through their charity work further embodied the essence of giving second chances to others, particularly to those less fortunate.

The concept of second chances became a central theme in Patil's talks and public appearances. He and Jaan championed the idea that everyone, no matter their circumstances, deserved a second chance to make something beautiful of their lives.

Patil and Jaan's legacy extended far beyond their professional achievements in cricket and cinema. Together, they dedicated themselves to various philanthropic efforts, focusing on causes close to their hearts such as education for underprivileged children and healthcare initiatives. Their foundation, known for its transparency and impactful projects, became a model of celebrity-driven charity work, earning them respect and admiration not only from their fans but also within the broader community. Their shared vision and collective efforts in giving back to society helped them carve out a deeply meaningful role as advocates for change, making their legacy a powerful testament to the idea that success truly shines when paired with a purpose to serve others.

In their golden years, surrounded by family and friends, and respected by a world that had watched them overcome adversities Yuvraj Patil and Jaan Kapur-Patil lived out their days in contentment. Their love story, born from the ashes of despair, served as an enduring symbol of life's capacity to offer second chances, beautifully illustrating how the most challenging moments can lead to the most rewarding chapters. Their journey, marked by resilience and renewed hope, remained a powerful reminder that life, in its complexity, often saves its best parts for the second act.

Despite facing significant personal losses that could have derailed his career, Patil's resolve only strengthened, illustrating his capacity to transform adversity into opportunity. His comeback century, celebrated in front of a home crowd, was not just a display of his sporting prowess but a declaration of his comeback in life. This pivotal moment marked a new beginning in his career and personal life, with his marriage to Jaan further symbolizing his belief in new beginnings.

Patil's journey is a compelling narrative of triumph over trials, underscoring the profound impact of resilience and the power of embracing second chances for a rebirth in both spirit and action.

51

CHAPTER FOUR

Entangled Affections

In the rustic outskirts of Visakhapatnam, surrounded by rolling hills and scattered villages, the elite International School of Architecture and Design stood as a beacon of modern education amidst the pastoral beauty. It was here, amid the low, terracotta-tiled buildings and sprawling green campus, that Marilyn first crossed paths with Rahul.

Marilyn, a curious and bright student with a penchant for cultural history, was immediately drawn to Rahul, a quiet and thoughtful boy whose creativity seemed boundless. Rahul, whose father's diplomatic career took their family across various continents, had a vision influenced by the diverse cultures he'd experienced. This background fueled his dream of creating architectural designs that could bridge cultures and foster unity.

Their friendship blossomed through countless hours spent in the art studio, which was filled with the scent of wet clay and paint, and the sounds of soft music mingling with creative chatter. Rahul's sketches of futuristic buildings-inspired by his travels to cities like Tokyo, Istanbul, and New York-covered the walls of the studio. These designs were not just buildings but symbols of cultural fusion, featuring elements like Japanese torii gates melded with Ottoman domes and skyscrapers adorned with intricate Indian jali work.

Marilyn, ever mischievous, would often hide Rahul's pencils to draw his attention.

Rahul: "Hey! I was using that!"

Marilyn: "Oh really? Could've fooled me with how slow you're moving!"

Rahul: (chasing her around) "That's because someone keeps distracting me!"

This led to spirited chases around the classroom, their laughter echoing off the walls, leaving a memory of youthful affection.

Marilyn, with her deep appreciation for the stories embedded in architectural forms, became Rahul's most avid supporter, encouraging him to blend his visions into tangible forms. She often brought books on art history from around the world, pointing out details that could enhance his designs, turning their sessions into a fusion of art, history, and imagination.

Their playful interactions, from light-hearted debates over the aesthetics of modernism versus postmodernism to collaborative projects for school exhibitions, were highlights of their school days. These moments not only deepened their bond but also anchored a lifelong friendship that would eventually see them exploring real-world projects that echoed their childhood dreams.

Their tender romance culminated at the school fair, an event filled with games and gaiety. Rahul, wanting to impress Marilyn, participated in every game booth until he won a plush teddy bear at the ring toss. Rahul nervously clutched the plush bear he had won for her, hesitating as he handed it over with a shy smile.

Rahul: "For you, Marilyn. I hope it's as soft as your smile."

Marilyn: (hugging the bear) "It's perfect. But not as perfect as this moment."

As the sun dipped below the horizon, the fairground adjacent to their school came alive with twinkling lights, echoing laughter, and the distant melodies of carnival music. The annual school fair, a much-anticipated event, was in full swing, transforming the usually tranquil grounds into a vibrant festival of colors and sounds. It was the perfect backdrop for youthful exuberance and budding romance.

Marilyn and Rahul, now in their senior year, wandered through the fair, hand in hand, their hearts full of the impending sorrow of graduation and the inevitable separation that would follow. Rahul was set to follow in his father's footsteps and move abroad for his architecture studies, while Marilyn planned to stay in India, delving deeper into art history and cultural studies. The reality that their paths were about to diverge cast a bittersweet shadow over their evening.

Amidst the chaos of the fair-between the laughter of their friends and the competitive shouts from the game booths-Rahul led Marilyn to a quieter corner, under a canopy of fairy lights. The lights, gentle and soft, cast a warm glow around them, creating an island of serenity. It was here that Rahul, his heart heavy with the thought of leaving, stole a sweet kiss from Marilyn. It was a kiss filled with the promise of remembrance and the hope of reunion, sealing their youthful love.

Their friends, having discreetly followed them, burst into cheers and jubilation, their claps and whistles piercing the night air, adding a layer of communal joy to the personal moment. Yet, beneath the celebration, both Rahul and Marilyn felt the sting of upcoming separation-a moment of joy frozen by the chilling winds of reality that whispered of months and years apart. This kiss, under the fairy lights, became a cherished memory, a symbol of their love that would need to endure time and distance.

As the school year ended, so did the chapter that had once defined Marilyn's world. Rahul left for his studies abroad, and though they promised to stay in touch, life's shifting rhythms slowly widened the space between them. Letters grew shorter, calls less frequent, and eventually, silence became the language of what once was. The ache of distance lingered in Marilyn's heart, but so did the warmth of a first love-untouched by bitterness, only preserved by time.

It was in this quiet space of change and growing self-discovery that Marilyn stepped into college life-eager to embrace new ideas, unsure if her heart was ready for anything more. And then came Robin.

He entered Marilyn's world with a reputation that preceded him. Known across campus for his sharp wit and eloquent speeches, Robin was a law student who carried himself with a distinctive air of confidence. His father, a renowned journalist celebrated for exposing injustices and championing the truth, had instilled in him a deep-rooted passion for justice and the courage to speak truth to power. Robin's presence was undeniable-felt in every classroom, every debate, every conversation that mattered.

Marilyn met him during a guest lecture on the interplay between cultural heritage and legal frameworks. Robin's insightful questions and bold perspectives caught her attention, not with the innocence that once defined her bond with Rahul, but with the intrigue of something deeper, more cerebral. What began as casual admiration soon grew into a connection-an intellectual current neither expected, yet both welcomed. Their courtship became an exhilarating blend of mind and spirit, filled with long discussions on everything from legal ethics to the philosophical underpinnings of modern art.

Their dates often included spontaneous adventures-visiting art exhibitions at local galleries, attending theater premieres, or engaging in spirited debates at coffee shops, where they would lose track of time. Robin's dynamic personality complemented Marilyn's thoughtful nature, challenging her views and expanding her horizons. He introduced her to legal documentaries and classic novels, while she brought him closer to the world of art, helping him appreciate the narratives embedded in sculptures and paintings.

Despite the intellectual rigor of their interactions, their relationship was also filled with lighthearted moments. Robin's quick humor and penchant for impromptu poetry readings made Marilyn laugh in a way she hadn't since her days with Rahul. Their connection was a tapestry woven from threads of mutual respect, shared passions, and the exhilarating rush of discovering life through each other's eyes. This dynamic interplay of stimulation and fun made their courtship a deeply enriching chapter in Marilyn's life, as she navigated the complexities of love and learning in her college years.

They often engaged in spirited debates, challenging each other's viewpoints which stretched late into the night, surrounded by law books and notes.

Robin: "If love were a crime, you'd be guilty as charged."
Marilyn: "And you'd defend me, of course?"

Robin: "To the very end. But only if the jury is as charmed by you as I am."

Robin, knowing Marilyn's penchant for puzzles, would create elaborate scavenger hunts across campus, each clue cleverly crafted to reveal the time and place of their next rendezvous.

They were a common sight in the mock trial sessions at the university, where Robin, ever the debater, defended Marilyn against mock charges ranging from "stealing his heart" to "hoarding too many library books."

Their mock trial antics often left their peers in stitches, blending their romance with campus lore.

Marilyn: (pretending to be solemn) "I plead guilty to stealing too many glances during your closing argument."

Robin: (grinning) "The punishment must fit the crime. How about dinner with the defending counsel?"

These moments were interspersed with laughter and deep, meaningful exchanges that fortified their bond beyond mere romantic interest.

Their relationship was as much about mental stimulation as it was about affection.

The separation between Marilyn and Robin was inevitable, yet deeply painful. They had shared a connection that transcended the ordinary-a love built not only on affection but on the mental and emotional depth that came from hours of conversation, shared dreams, and moments of laughter that lingered long after. They had challenged each other's intellect, sparking curiosity and new perspectives. Their talks delved into philosophy, dreams, and the very fabric of life, anchoring them in a world where they felt fully seen and heard.

But as time passed, life's practicalities pulled them in different directions. They had goals and responsibilities that neither could set aside, no matter how much they wanted to. There was an unspoken understanding between them, a silent resignation that this parting was necessary, even if neither had the heart to say it outright.

On their last evening together, they walked side by side, wrapped in a bittersweet silence. Words felt unnecessary; they simply absorbed the fleeting moment, hoping to freeze it in time. When it came time to say goodbye, there was no grand gesture, no declaration of love-just a lingering touch, a look that held all the things they couldn't say, and a quiet promise to never forget.

They separated not out of a lack of love but out of respect for the path each had to take. And though their lives would go on, the memory of their connection would forever remain etched in their hearts, a testament to the beauty of a relationship that had been as much about soul as it was about romance.

As Marilyn transitioned into her role in her father's expansive business empire, her path crossed with Ranbir, a creative and passionate chef who had inherited a zest for life from his father, the head of the National Culinary Board (NCB). Their meeting occurred at one of Ranbir's cooking classes, intended to fuse traditional Flavors with modern techniques. Their mutual love for food and innovation sparked an immediate connection.

Their courtship was marked by culinary battles in Ranbir's kitchen, where they challenged each other to create exquisite dishes under a ticking clock, their competitive spirits fuelled by flirtatious banter.

In the heat of Ranbir's kitchen, their competitive spirit often turned into flirty exchanges over sizzling pans.

Ranbir: "I hope you like spicy, because this dish is as fiery as you are tonight."

Marilyn: "Is that so? Maybe I'll have to cool it down with my signature dessert."

Ranbir introduced Marilyn to the magic of midnight picnics on the restaurant's rooftop, where they sampled each other's creations under a canopy of stars, the city lights a dim backdrop to their secluded dining. Each dish they shared was a testament to their growing affection, each bite a blend of love and culinary art.

One night, while enjoying their rooftop picnic, Marilyn's emotions bubbled over with the perfect combination of ambiance and Ranbir's thoughtful gestures. Marilyn: "This is beautiful, Ranbir. You've really outdone yourself."

Ranbir: "Only the best for you. Every dish tastes better with you here."

Their laughter mingled with the clinking of glasses, each course drawing them closer in the serene night, their conversation turning from culinary arts to dreams and Marilyn's journey through her relationships with Rahul, Robin, and Ranbir became the compass guiding her through the depths of her own soul. Each romance was a unique chapter, contributing to the mosaic of her life in ways that were as transformative as they were unforgettable.

Rahul was her first love, the kind that swept her off her feet with its innocence and intensity. With him, she learned about vulnerability and trust. His warmth and stability made her feel safe, giving her the courage to open her heart fully for the first time. Though they eventually grew apart, her relationship with Rahul taught her the value of sincerity and the bittersweet beauty of young love-a memory she would hold dear.

Robin entered her life like a whirlwind, challenging her intellect and expanding her horizons. Their bond was as much a meeting of minds as it was of hearts. Through him, Marilyn discovered the thrill of mental stimulation and the importance of having a partner who could understand and inspire her on an intellectual level. Their conversations were intense, thought-provoking, and left her wanting more. Even after they parted, Marilyn carried with her a newfound sense of self, a confidence in her own intelligence and ideas, realizing she could seek a partner who would encourage her to be her true self.

Ranbir was different-a wild, passionate force that lit up her world in ways she hadn't imagined. He pushed her out of her comfort zone, inspiring her to live more freely, embracing spontaneity and adventure. With him, Marilyn discovered the joy of living in the moment, feeling fully alive, and embracing the beauty of imperfection. Ranbir's unpredictable nature showed her that love wasn't always logical, that sometimes, it was the unpredictable twists and turns that made life meaningful.

Each relationship Marilyn experienced was more than just a chapter in her life-it was a mirror reflecting parts of herself she had yet to discover. With every bond, she peeled back another layer of her heart, uncovering strengths she didn't know she possessed and fears she hadn't dared to face. Rahul taught her the quiet power of tenderness, Robin challenged her to think deeper and dream bolder, and Ranbir ignited her spirit with spontaneity and joy. Their love, their laughter, even their partings-each moment left a fingerprint on her soul.

She didn't emerge unscarred, but she emerged more whole.

These were not just fleeting romances; they were transformative experiences that shaped her inner world. Through them, Marilyn came to see herself more clearly-not as someone merely searching for love, but as a woman learning what it meant to truly love herself. Each heartache, each high, each hesitation brought her closer to understanding what she desired-not just in a partner, but in life, in purpose, in her place in the world.

And in that understanding, something beautiful began to bloom: the quiet confidence of a woman who had lived, learned, and was finally ready to love without losing herself.

Marilyn's journey into love and relationships was shaped long before she ever experienced them firsthand, rooted in the shadow of her mother's deeply ingrained distrust. Growing up, Marilyn observed her mother's constant, almost ritualistic suspicion towards her father, a successful business tycoon whose work frequently took him on trips, often accompanied by female colleagues and staff. To Marilyn's mother, these trips were a breeding ground for betrayal, filling her with an anxious vigilance that cast a quiet tension over their household. Subtle comments, lingering glances at his schedule, and a faint but persistent air of distrust became part of Marilyn's daily reality.

Unconsciously, Marilyn absorbed this atmosphere as a fundamental aspect of relationships. To her young mind, suspicion and love were intertwined; this vigilance felt as normal as affection or care. The family dynamic left her with an underlying belief that distrust was not just a reaction to infidelity but a necessary element to "guard" love, to prevent it from slipping away.

As she ventured into her own relationships, the echoes of her mother's behavior began to manifest. Despite her partners' varied personalities-a passionate creative, a rational lawyer, and finally a compassionate doctor-Marilyn fell into a predictable, tragic rhythm. Each relationship began with the hope of connection, a promise of shared dreams and mutual trust. But, almost inevitably, she would find herself consumed by doubt, looking for signs of betrayal, convinced that hidden disloyalty lurked beneath the surface.

Her suspicions, though often unfounded, became a silent antagonist, surfacing in conversations and private moments. She would scrutinize innocent remarks, question small details, and read meaning into things that didn't exist. For her partners, the cycle was exhausting; they struggled to reassure her, to ease her insecurities, but the constant strain eventually became overwhelming. Despite their best efforts, they found themselves unable to bear the weight of Marilyn's internal battle with trust. In time, each relationship unraveled, leaving Marilyn isolated, with a painful sense of déjà vu and a lingering question of whether true love could ever break the pattern her mother had unwittingly instilled.

Through these experiences, Marilyn began to recognize the toll that suspicion had taken on her life, both personally and romantically. Yet, this self-awareness was not enough to break free from the cycle entirely, as she found herself continuously caught in a web of distrust that had become all too familiar, a tragic echo of her mother's own fears.

After watching Marilyn endure a series of heartbreaks, her parents-worried and weary-began to believe that perhaps love, on its own, wasn't enough to anchor her. In a bid to offer her a steadier future, they arranged a marriage with a doctor, someone they believed possessed not just professional stability but also the calm temperament and emotional intelligence needed to understand her inner turmoil. To them, his medical background symbolized care, patience, and an ability to heal-not just the body, but perhaps the lingering wounds Marilyn carried quietly within. They hoped that in his presence, she might finally find the balance and peace that had long eluded her.

However, the presence of a caring and committed husband did not alter Marilyn's ingrained patterns of suspicion. Her husband's late hours at the hospital, necessary for his profession, were misinterpreted by Marilyn as opportunities for infidelity. Phone calls that extended into the night, part of his medical duties, were seen as clandestine conversations. This constant scrutiny subjected their marriage to severe stress, challenging the doctor's patience and compassion.

Despite the turmoil, her husband's suggestion of therapy became a pivotal point in Marilyn's life. Therapy offered her insights into her behavior, tracing the roots back to her childhood. Understanding that her reactions were more a learned response than reality, Marilyn began the challenging work of unlearning these patterns. Therapy provided her a space to explore her insecurities and gradually start to dismantle the defensive mechanisms she had built over the years.

This journey was neither quick nor easy, filled with setbacks as each small trigger threatened to undo progress. However, it was also a path marked by small triumphs, as Marilyn learned to trust not just her husband but also herself. As she healed, her relationships-both with her husband and others around her-began to change, reflecting her inner growth. Her story illustrates the painful yet powerful transformation possible when one confronts and works through deep-seated personal issues, highlighting the impact of childhood experiences on adult relationships and the redemptive power of therapy and personal effort in overcoming them.

In the newfound calm of therapy and self-reflection, Marilyn began to reshape her perception of love and trust. Her husband, the doctor, proved to be not just a caretaker in the traditional sense but a steadfast partner in her journey towards healing. His unwavering support during her therapy sessions and his gentle reassurance in times of doubt gradually helped rebuild the fragile trust that had shattered in her previous relationships.

As Marilyn gradually confronted her inner fears, she began to recognize the early signs of doubt before they took control. With therapy and self-awareness, she learned to pause, reflect, and separate past wounds from present realities. This shift allowed her to truly see her husband's unwavering care-not as suspect, but as sincere. His late nights and long hours became symbols of dedication, not distance, and for the first time, Marilyn responded with trust instead of fear.

Their relationship blossomed with quiet grace, shaped by Marilyn's healing and her husband's gentle patience. His steady presence, the way he listened without judgment and touched her with quiet affection, became the comfort she had long craved. In his arms, she felt safe enough to be vulnerable. Slowly, love began to bloom-not rushed or dramatic, but tender and true-rooted in understanding, and deepened by the soft moments they now shared without fear.

On quiet evenings at home, they would sit side by side, sharing stories from their pasts, memories that had once seemed distant now finding a place in the warmth of their present. Marilyn often spoke of her childhood, the laughter and comfort of simpler days, but also the hidden fears that had grown unnoticed. The doctor would listen, nodding with understanding, sometimes sharing similar memories of his own-a family gathering, a small-town festival, a quiet day fishing with his father. They would talk about how those moments shaped them, leaving each with a stronger sense of their own paths and dreams.

Sometimes, over a glass of wine, they would laugh at the sillier moments they'd had in previous relationships, sharing memories that felt both funny and bittersweet. Marilyn would tell him about the impulsive road trip she'd once taken with Rahul, getting lost but refusing to admit it, navigating back on sheer instinct and a printed map. The doctor would laugh, sharing his own story of a failed cooking experiment he had once attempted to impress an ex.

These conversations, so open and light, carried a kind of nostalgic weight, bringing them closer and creating a foundation of trust they had each longed for.

Their bond also began to spill over into Marilyn's professional life. She found herself more present, no longer hindered by the lingering shadows of insecurity that had once held her back. Her colleagues noticed the change-a confidence in her voice, an ease in her smile that hadn't been there before. Where she had once second-guessed her decisions or avoided certain interactions, she now took the lead, engaging openly, unafraid of judgment or doubt.

In conversations with her work friends, she sometimes found herself sharing little glimpses of her life with her doctor husband. A funny anecdote from a Sunday brunch, a spontaneous weekend trip to the mountains, or the quiet joy of an evening spent reading together by the fire. Her friends would smile knowingly, noticing the soft glow in her eyes, the subtle shift in her tone. Marilyn's transformation had become evident not just to her but to everyone around her, inspiring warmth and a newfound camaraderie with those she worked with.

Each conversation they shared, each quiet moment filled with laughter or reflection, slowly became threads in the fabric of Marilyn's life-a rich, evolving tapestry stitched with love, self-discovery, and healing. Whether it was a spontaneous road trip, a simple dinner at home, or a vulnerable confession exchanged in the stillness of night, these memories layered themselves gently over old wounds, softening them with the warmth of something real and lasting.

As Marilyn reflected on the path that had brought her here-from the innocence of first love to the turbulence of heartbreak, and finally to the calm embrace of a love rooted in trust-she felt something shift within her. It wasn't just gratitude for the man who stood beside her, steady and kind. It was also a profound appreciation for the journey itself-the mistakes, the lessons, the painful truths she'd had to confront in order to grow. For the first time, she didn't just believe in love; she felt worthy of it. And in that quiet realization, her heart felt full-of peace, of purpose, and of a love she could finally call her own.

The vow renewal ceremony unfolded like a dream-soft, intimate, and drenched in meaning. Every detail, from the subtle arrangements of white lilies to the mellow glow of the string lights swaying under a starlit sky, was imbued with the essence of their love's quiet rebirth. Friends and family gathered not merely to witness a ritual but to celebrate a journey-one marked by endurance, forgiveness, and growth. They knew, perhaps more than anyone, the trials that had led Marilyn and her husband to this moment.

As Marilyn stood facing him, the man who had walked beside her through storms she could barely name, she felt a swell of emotion rise within her. There was no nervous flutter, no hesitation-only a deep, resonant stillness that came with knowing she was exactly where she was meant to be. His eyes, steady and warm, searched hers not for answers, but for recognition-for the love that had survived, evolved, and deepened with time.

When he reached for her hand, his touch grounded her, yet awakened something electric inside-a spark of desire not dulled by the years, but refined by them. As they recited their vows, it felt like breathing life into a love that had been tested, stretched, and ultimately reaffirmed. Each word fell like a tender whisper between them, echoing a promise not of perfection, but of partnership. His thumb traced slow, soothing circles on her palm, and she could feel the quiet fire in his gaze-a fire that reminded her how far they had come, and how fiercely he had stayed.

Later that night, as the music faded and the guests scattered into laughter-filled groups, they stole away into the moonlight. Beneath the hushed silver glow, away from the watchful eyes of the world, they found a moment just for themselves. No longer needing grand gestures, their bodies spoke the language of reunion-the brush of his fingers along her cheek, the way her breath hitched as he pulled her close, the pulse of shared memories that made their embrace feel both new and achingly familiar.

The passion between them wasn't the fevered rush of new love, but the burn of something earned-seasoned by time, scarred by past pains, and nurtured into something enduring. That night, they loved each other with the kind of intimacy that only comes from healing together-raw, real, and profoundly tender.

Their relationship blossomed as Marilyn's heart opened, revealing a side of her that had long been hidden beneath layers of doubt. The ceremony didn't just mark a renewal of vows; it marked the culmination of a journey. One that began with a young girl, shaped by her mother's quiet fears and haunted by the shadows of mistrust. A girl who had long associated love with doubt, and affection with anxiety. A girl who, through a series of tangled affections, had searched for connection in all its forms-first in the innocence of Rahul, then the intellectual spark of Robin, and later, the wild charm of Ranbir. Each had touched her, each had taught her, and each had revealed fragments of who she was and what she needed.

But it was only through confronting her deepest fears that Marilyn finally began to unravel the web that had quietly entangled her for years. Therapy didn't change her overnight-but it opened a door she had never dared to walk through: the door of self-awareness. And on the other side, she didn't find perfection, but progress. Her husband's unwavering support-his patience, his quiet encouragement-gave her the space to grow. Slowly, she learned to trust not just him, but herself.

Marilyn and her doctor continued to grow side by side, their love enriched by the journey they'd taken together. They were no longer the people they'd been when they first met. They were stronger, braver, and more open-hearted, with a bond that had been forged through resilience and unconditional support. Marilyn's newfound self-assurance transformed not only her marriage but her life as a whole. She became a light to those around her, embodying the wisdom and compassion she had gained, inspiring friends, family, and colleagues who saw in her the power of true change.

In the end, their love story was more than just a romance. It was a celebration of second chances, a reminder that no matter how deep the scars or how complex the past, the heart has an incredible capacity to heal, to learn, and to grow. Through their journey, they proved that love, when paired with dedication and understanding, can transform even the deepest wounds into sources of strength. Together, they had crafted a life full of harmony, joy, and purpose, embracing a future that was not only a second chance but a culmination of the love and resilience they had so beautifully built.

CHAPTER FIVE

BEYOND BOUNDARIES

Hemant gripped the handles of his father's old scooter, weaving through the bustling streets of Karnal, a small town shadowed by the vast expanse of Delhi's metropolis. The scooter, a relic from his father's youthful days, sputtered along, mirroring Hemant's own journey from humble beginnings to the prestigious corridors of the Indian Institute of Management (IIM) Kolkata.

From an early age, Hemant's intellect set him apart. He was the boy who puzzled over numbers and patterns instead of playing cricket in the dusty lanes of his neighborhood. His razor-sharp mind first turned heads when, at the tender age of twelve, he not only participated in but clinched a national Math Olympiad, solving complex problems that baffled even seasoned teachers. This victory was not just a win; it was a revelation of his potential to his family and to himself.

Academically voracious, Hemant's journey through school was marked by a string of accolades. Yet, it was his pragmatic approach to his studies, focusing on practical applications and real-world impact, that truly distinguished him. His family's traditional values-emphasizing stability, respect, and diligence-shaped his worldview, urging him to pursue a career that promised not just personal success but also familial pride.

The admission to IIM Kolkata was more than an academic achievement; it was the culmination of years of disciplined study and the weight of his family's expectations resting firmly on his shoulders. As he maneuvered the scooter through Karnal, past the familiar sights and sounds of his youth, Hemant pondered the next phase of his life, unaware that soon, his carefully laid plans would be challenged not by market trends or business cases, but by the unpredictable whims of the heart.

Kopal stepped onto the IIM campus with a grace that belied the determined fire within her. Her youthful beauty, marked by delicate features and expressive eyes, turned heads, but it was her quiet confidence and poise that left a lasting impression. Growing up Durgapur town in Bengal, her life was steeped in cultural richness-festivals filled with colors, music that echoed through the balmy nights, and stories that wove through generations. Yet, beneath the vibrant cultural tapestry, her conservative family nurtured a traditional outlook that often felt constricting.

From a young age, Kopal displayed an innate empathy and a passion for understanding the human condition, traits that often put her at odds with the expectations set before her. Her decision to pursue a career in management was met with reservations from her family, who feared it might lead her too far from their values and traditions. But Kopal, with her quiet strength, pursued her dreams relentlessly. She worked hard, balancing respect for her heritage with her ambitions, and ultimately earned a coveted spot at IIM.

At IIM, Kopal blossomed intellectually and personally, her empathetic nature and keen insights into human behavior making her a beloved figure among peers and professors alike. She navigated her courses and extracurricular activities with elan, championing causes close to her heart and often bridging gaps between disparate groups on campus. Her presence was a blend of traditional elegance and modern independence, making her a figure of inspiration and intrigue among her classmates.

As she walked through the corridors, her saree gently swaying with each step, Kopal carried with her the dreams of her small-town upbringing intertwined with the ambitions of her newfound independence. It was in this setting of academic pursuit and personal discovery that her path would cross with Hemant's, setting the stage for a convergence of minds and hearts that would challenge both their planned trajectories.

Hemant and Kopal's initial meeting at the college reunion event unfolded like a scene from a beautifully orchestrated play. Amidst the laughter and reminiscences of former classmates, their introduction was a quiet moment that marked the beginning of something extraordinary. Hemant, usually reserved, found himself drawn to the warmth radiating from Kopal's smile and the thoughtful intensity in her eyes. She, in turn, sensed a reassuring calm in his demeanor, a stability that intrigued her amidst the boisterous reunions.

As the evening progressed, their conversation flowed effortlessly, bridging topics from classic literature to contemporary issues in management. Each found in the other a surprising depth and a shared intellectual curiosity that deepened their connection. Hemant, who had always viewed relationships through a pragmatic lens, began to experience a shift in his perceptions, feeling the contours of his well-defined worldviews softening in the glow of Kopal's empathetic presence.

Kopal, equally moved by their burgeoning friendship, admired Hemant's methodical approach to life and his deep respect for tradition, which resonated with her own cultural roots. Their friendship blossomed against the backdrop of alumni gatherings and late-night campus walks, each encounter weaving a tighter bond between them. As they shared stories of their childhoods, their dreams, and occasionally, their doubts, a mutual understanding and respect took root.

This growing connection prompted Hemant to confront his preconceived notions about love and partnership. He found himself questioning the cultural scripts he had unconsciously adhered to all his life. With Kopal, the concept of building a life together seemed not just a merging of paths but a beautiful exploration of new horizons. Their relationship, born from a meeting of minds at a college reunion, gradually evolved into a profound exploration of what it means to love, respect, and truly understand someone from a seemingly different world.

As Hemant and Kopal's relationship deepened, they both faced the inevitable challenge of bringing their families into their shared world. Each family held reservations, steeped in concerns about cultural integrity and the challenges of intercultural marriage.

One evening, Hemant sat down with his family in their living room, the air thick with tension as he broached the subject.

Hemant: "Maa, Papa, there is something important I need to discuss with you. I have met someone special at the reunion. Her name is Kopal."

Father: "Kopal? That doesn't sound like a name from our community. Where is she from?"

Hemant: "She is from Bengal. I know this might come as a surprise, but we have grown very close. She is kind, intelligent, and respects our values."

Mother: "Hemant, we've always trusted your judgment, but marriage is not just about two people. It's about bringing two families, two cultures together. Are you sure she will fit into our ways?"

Hemant: "I understand your concerns, but I believe what Kopal and I share transcends these differences. I've seen her respect and embrace our traditions whenever she's been with me."

Father: "It's not just about respect, Hemant. It's about living those traditions, passing them on. How certain are you that our traditions will be upheld?"

Hemant: "I am confident, Papa. We've discussed this at length. We are committed to blending our traditions, to learning from each other."

The conversation was filled with a mix of concern and genuine curiosity, with Hemant patiently addressing each worry, hoping to bridge the gap between his love for Kopal and his loyalty to his family's expectations.

Meanwhile, Kopal faced her own set of challenges, as she sat down with her family in their traditional home in Bengal.

Kopal: "Baba, Ma, there is someone in my life. His name is Hemant, and he is from Karnal."

Mother: "Karnal? That's quite far, Kopal. And what about our customs, our culture? Will he understand? Will he respect where you come from?"

Kopal: "He does, Ma. Hemant is a wonderful man, grounded in his own culture yet open to mine. He respects me and everything that makes me who I am."

Father: "But Kopal, these cultural differences are not small matters. They shape our everyday lives. How do you plan to navigate them in your daily life, especially when it comes to your future children?"

Kopal: "We've talked about it a lot, Baba. We intend to give our children a rich blend of both cultures. We believe it will make them more understanding, more enriched individuals."

Her parents listened, their expressions a mix of skepticism and hope, as Kopal made her case with heartfelt sincerity.

Both Hemant and Kopal faced the delicate task of not only defending their love but also painting a picture of a shared future that honored both of their backgrounds. The conversations were not just about assurances, but about forging understanding and respect between the families, emphasizing the beauty of their union rather than the differences that marked their origins.

Together, as they navigate the complexities of balancing family expectations with their own dreams, determined to stay united despite the obstacles, both land coveted positions at a top multinational firm, where their skills are recognized and valued. Soon after joining, they're given an exciting but challenging offer-transfers to the company's headquarters in the United States. Eager to embrace the adventure and knowing this would give them time to build their life together, they accept the transfer.

Arriving in the U.S., they experience both thrill and uncertainty as they settle into a new country and a new phase of their relationship. The distance from home, however, also gives them a newfound freedom from traditional expectations and family pressures. Hemant and Kopal grow closer, their relationship blossoming without the constraints of their cultural differences weighing on them daily. In the quiet corners of their shared apartment, they decide to marry, just the two of them, making promises to love and support each other no matter what comes.

Their wedding Is simple and intimate, a quiet courthouse ceremony followed by a romantic dinner. They feel a blend of joy and a tinge of guilt as they keep the marriage secret from their families. For now, they want to focus on their careers and their partnership without the concerns and judgments they know will follow when their families learn the news. It's a decision made in love but one that they know cannot stay hidden forever.

On one of the quiet evenings, the couple were enjoying a moment in their garden.

Hemant: (pulling Kopal close) "You know, every day with you feels like our first day together, full of new surprises and endless love."

Kopal: (resting her head on his shoulder) "And every night with you feels like a dream I never want to wake from."

Hemant: "I promise to keep dreaming with you, to keep building our dreams into reality, one day at a time."

Kopal: "And I promise to always find new ways to fall in love with you, over and over."

Months pass, and their lives flourish both at work and at home. Then, one chilly autumn morning, Kopal surprises Hemant with news that changes everything-she's pregnant. Shocked and overjoyed, Hemant holds her close, realizing how much this new life cements their bond. Despite their happiness, they grapple with the knowledge that this secret they share will soon need to become known. Yet, before they can even begin to plan how to tell their families, life has another surprise in store: they're having twins.

As the months roll by, their excitement grows along with the quiet realization that they're stepping into a new role-becoming a family. When the time finally comes, their twins enter the world, a baby girl with big, curious eyes, whom they name Chumki, and a baby boy with an infectious smile, named Chunmun. Holding their children for the first time, Hemant and Kopal feel a profound love and responsibility, not only for each other but for the small lives now depending on them.

With their twins in their arms, Hemant knows it's time to share the news. Though he dreads the reaction, he feels he owes it to his parents to be honest. One evening, he sits in the quiet of their living room, mustering the courage to make the call to his parents back in India. His heart pounds as he dials, knowing that this conversation will forever change their family dynamics.

As his parent's answer, he starts with simple pleasantries, asking about their health and updating them on his work. After a few moments of small talk, he takes a deep breath and speaks the truth: "Mom, Dad, there's something I need to tell you. I got married- to Kopal. And... we just had twins. A girl, Chumki, and a boy, Chunmun."

There's a long, tense silence on the other end of the line. His parents are stunned, their reaction a mix of shock, disbelief, and a complicated blend of emotions that Hemant can't quite decipher. When his father finally speaks, his voice is soft but stern. "Why did you keep this from us, Hemant? We thought you trusted us."

The words sting, and Hemant explains how he and Kopal feared that their families wouldn't accept their relationship, how they wanted to build a life without the strain of judgment or expectations. His mother's silence cuts through him, but she finally speaks, her voice breaking as she asks about her grandchildren.

Despite the initial shock and hurt, his parents' natural warmth for their new grandchildren softens the conversation. They begin asking questions about the twins, from how Chumki and Chunmun look to when they'll get to see them.

Hemant senses that, while there is still hurt to heal, his parents are beginning to accept the reality of his life with Kopal.

Over the next few months, Hemant and Kopal work to rebuild the relationship with their families, gradually drawing them into their lives across continents. Slowly as years passed, the family come to terms with their decision, welcoming Chumki and Chunmun into the fold with joy and affection. They may have started "Beyond Boundaries," but Hemant and Kopal's love has now brought their families together in ways they had never imagined.

Hemant: (laughing) "Kopal, look! Chunmun is trying to outdo Chumki in who can make the bigger tower with their blocks."

Kopal: (smiling, calling out to the twins) "Be careful, little architects! The living room is not a construction site!"

Chumki: (giggling, knocking over her brother's tower) "My tower stands tallest!"

Chunmun: (pretending to be upset but quickly rebuilding) "It's okay, I'll make one that touches the sky!"

Kopal: "And I'll be the first to visit the sky tower. But only if there's a promise of cookies at the top!"

Despite the initial shock, Kopal also prepares herself to break the news to her stepparents back in Bengal. They react with devastation; she is their only daughter, and they had many dreams for her future. To Kopal's face, they show happiness and acceptance, congratulating her on her new family. But behind her back, they hatch a plan to bring their daughter back to India permanently.

After a year of keeping up appearances, her father calls her urgently, claiming her mother is on her deathbed. Heartbroken and worried, Kopal, accompanied by Hemant, rushes to India. Upon arrival, her stepparents play into local superstitions to manipulate and confine her to their ancestral home, using her deep-rooted cultural beliefs to their advantage.

Meanwhile, Hemant, who returns to the U.S. briefly for work, tries to stay in touch, but communication suddenly stops. Frantic, he calls her parents, only to be told a fabricated story that Kopal died in an accident while they were visiting a hill station. Devastated, Hemant's parents rush to Bengal, but they find no trace of Kopal or any accident report. They file a police complaint, sparking an investigation into her supposed death.

Unknown to them, Kopal is kept hidden in a supposedly haunted bungalow on the outskirts of her hometown.

Kopal feels uneasy as her stepparents begin performing superstitions around her.

Kopal: (confused and scared) "Why are you drawing that circle around me?"

Stepfather: "It's for your protection, dear. We need to make sure no evil spirits harm you."

Kopal: "But I don't understand. What spirits? I just came here to see mom."

Stepmother: (sinisterly) "Sometimes, dear, it's the spirits we can't see that we need protection from the most."

Under the influence of local superstitions and psychological manipulation, she is forced into a sham marriage with a man from a nearby village, orchestrated by her stepparents who seek to sever her ties with her previous life.

Hemant, unsettled by his suspicions and eager to ensure Kopal's safety, actively collaborates with the Indian police from the U.S. He reaches out to the authorities, explaining his concerns about Kopal's stepparents, who he suspects may be involved in illegal activities that could endanger Kopal. Leveraging his professional networks, Hemant arranges a meeting with a senior police official through video conferencing. He presents a detailed account of Kopal's interactions with her stepparents, highlighting specific incidents that raised his suspicions.

Hemant also provides evidence he has quietly gathered, such as financial irregularities he noticed in the family business and Kopal's own apprehensions. Recognizing the gravity of the situation, the police agree to discreetly monitor the stepparents' activities. They initiate a low-profile investigation, conducting background checks and surveilling their business operations without alerting them. Hemant stays in regular contact with the police, receiving updates and providing further information as needed, showing his deep commitment to Kopal's well-being and safety.

The investigation intensifies, and police track the stepparents' movements to the remote bungalow. As they raid the hideout, Kopal's children, brought by Hemant as part of the investigation, instantly recognize their mother. The sight and sound of her children help Kopal snap out of the coerced state she's been living in.

The stepparents and the man who was forced to marry Kopal are arrested for abduction and coercion. With the truth revealed, Hemant takes his family back to Delhi. There, his parents, overjoyed to see Kopal alive and well, openly condemn the superstitions and actions of her stepparents. They embrace their daughter-in-law and grandchildren, celebrating their return.

Having faced such a harrowing ordeal, Hemant and Kopal decide to give life a second chance back in the U.S., reaffirming their commitment to each other and their children. They leave for the U.S., hopeful and determined to rebuild their lives, free from the shadows of the past. Their love and resilience stand as a testament to their family's strength and unity, promising a future filled with hope and devoid of superstition.

As Hemant and Kopal prepare to leave India and head back to the U.S., they take a moment to reflect on the profound journey they have endured together. The night before their flight, they decide to visit their favourite spot in Delhi-a quiet, beautifully lit garden that holds special memories from the early days of their relationship. The garden, under the canopy of stars, is blooming with the fragrant scent of jasmine and the gentle rustle of leaves.

Hemant: (taking her hands) "Kopal, these past months were a storm, but standing here with you, I feel the calm returning to my world."

Kopal: (tearfully) "I was so lost, Hemant. The thought of you and our children kept me fighting to come back to you."

Hemant: "Nothing in this world could have kept me from finding you. Our love transcends all-distance, time, even the darkest magic."

Kopal: "Let's leave the darkness behind, Hemant. Let's bring only light into our lives, light and love."

Hemant: "Just light, love, and a thousand reasons to smile every day. Our story isn't about boundaries; it's about breaking them down, together."

Hemant takes Kopal's hand, leading her to a secluded bench where they first decided to build a life together. Sitting there, they look into each other's eyes, the weight of their recent trials making this moment of peace feel even more precious.

Hemant pulls a small box from his pocket and opens it to reveal a pair of custommade pendants, each half of a heart, inscribed with their initials. "No matter how far apart we might seem, we're always together. These have our past, our present, and our future," he says, his voice thick with emotion.

Kopal, moved by the gesture, feels tears well up in her eyes. She places her pendant around her neck and does the same for Hemant, their fingers lingering on each other's skin. "I never doubted us, not for a moment," she whispers back, her words a testament to their enduring love. Hemant draws her close, their foreheads touching gently. "You and I, we're proof that love knows no boundaries," he murmurs. They sit in silence, soaking in the serenity and the strength of their bond, each heart beating in rhythm with the other's.

As the night deepens, Hemant stands and extends his hand to Kopal. "Dance with me," he says, a playful smile spreading across his face. There's no music playing, but in their hearts, a melody of love and triumph rings clear. They dance under the moonlight, turning softly, each step a dance of resilience and hope.

Their dance slows, and Hemant leans in to kiss Kopal, a kiss that seals their promises and dreams. "To a new beginning, in a place where we're free to love, to grow, and to be ourselves, without fear," he says as they break apart, their eyes locked in a shared vision of the future.

The next day, as they board their plane back to the U.S., they carry with them not just the joy of their reunion but a renewed spirit of adventure. They know the road ahead will have its challenges, but together, they are ready to face whatever comes, bound not just by love, but by a deep, unbreakable connection that transcends all boundaries. As the plane takes off, they look out at the horizon, their hands entwined, ready to continue their journey- a journey not just of distance and time, but of heart and soul, forever exploring the limitless expanse of love.

Their story becomes a testament to love's ability to transcend cultural boundaries. Through resilience and compassion, they show that while love may face challenges, true partnership is built on mutual respect, adaptability, and shared dreams.

TWISTS OF FATE

Amidst a heavy monsoon downpour in Uttarakhand, the mountain skies roared, mirroring the chaos brewing in Maya's life. She stood by the window, watching torrents of rain cascade down the hillsides, and reflected on the tangled web of love and betrayal that had come to define her world.

Six years ago, Maya was married to Arjun, a man she had believed to be her soulmate. She had met him when she was just 19, and after a whirlwind romance, they married and started building a life together.

Maya and Arjun's relationship began as a whirlwind romance, filled with the promise of a new beginning and a shared future. Maya, a vibrant and ambitious young woman, met Arjun during a trekking expedition in the serene landscapes of Uttarakhand.

Arjun: (holds Maya's hands under the vast, starlit sky) "Do you see how the stars look tonight? I swear they shine because they know we're looking at them together." Maya: (smiling) "With you, every night feels like a starry one, even when it's cloudy."

Their connection was instantaneous and profound, sparked by shared interests and deep conversations under the vast, starlit skies. Arjun, with his easy charm and thoughtful nature, seemed like the perfect match for Maya, who longed for a partner who understood her dreams and passions.

Maya: (as they watch the sunset over the hills) "This view is beautiful." Arjun: "Not as beautiful as the sight of you every morning."

As their relationship deepened, Maya and Arjun found themselves entwined not just in the daylight hours of shared activities and responsibilities, but also in the mesmerizing dance of twilight entanglements. Each evening brought with it the promise of whispered conversations under starlit skies, where they explored the contours of their dreams and the depths of their fears. In these quiet hours, they learned the rhythms of each other's hearts, discovering an intimacy that was as profound as it was passionate. The twilight became their sacred time, lit by the soft glow of the moon and the flickering candles that Maya loved to light, creating a world that was uniquely theirs.

However, their initial euphoria began to encounter the inevitable trials of life. The challenges started as minor disagreements that could have been dismissed as the natural adjustments of any new marriage. Yet, these small issues gradually built up, revealing underlying tensions that neither Maya nor Arjun had anticipated. Their once serene twilights started to bear the weight of unresolved conflicts and unmet expectations, testing the resilience of their bond. As they navigated this complex terrain, they realized that the strength of their love would not just be measured by how they reveled in each other's company, but by how they faced the adversities that lay ahead.

Maya: "You forgot our anniversary, Arjun! How could you?" Arjun: "I'm sorry, Maya, there's just so much going on at work right now." Maya: "There's always something, isn't there?"

Maya: "You never listen to me anymore! It's like talking to a wall." Arjun: "I do listen, Maya, just not when you're yelling!"

Arjun still carried the shadows of his past, etched deeply within him. He and Rani had met during their first year of college, two eager spirits drawn together by a shared love for literature and late-night conversations under the starry sky. Rani, with her infectious laugh and boundless curiosity, had quickly become Arjun's entire world. They had wandered through the alleys of young love, dreaming of a future where they would explore the corners of the world together, hand in hand.

Their relationship had blossomed beautifully, filled with passionate debates, shared dreams, and quiet moments of vulnerability. Arjun had seen his future in Rani's eyes, and it had been bright and promising. He remembered the chilly winter evenings spent wrapped in a single blanket, talking about everything and nothing until the sun peeked above the horizon. He recalled the way her nose would crinkle when she laughed, and how she danced with abandon to her favorite songs, pulling him along into her joy.

But the intensity of their connection was matched by the pain of its ending. The day Rani told him about her acceptance to a prestigious university abroad, the world they had built together started to crumble. He had tried to be supportive, hiding his dread under a veneer of smiles and congratulations. The weeks leading up to her departure were a torturous countdown, each moment tinged with the bittersweet knowledge that their shared dreams were slipping through his fingers.

On their last day together, they had walked through the college campus in silence, each step heavy with unspoken sorrow. At the place where they had first met, Rani had turned to him, tears glistening in her eyes. "Don't forget me, Arjun," she had whispered, her voice breaking with the weight of their impending separation. The final goodbye had been a tearful embrace, a silent promise to hold on to what they had, even as destiny pulled them apart.

In the aftermath, Arjun's world had turned colorless. His journey through anguish, gloom, and nostalgia became an ordeal that tested him in profound ways. His once bright demeanor was overshadowed by a persistent gloom that clung to him like a heavy cloak. He would sit for hours staring out the window, lost in thoughts, as raindrops traced slow paths down the glass, mirroring the sadness in his eyes.

He threw himself Into his studies and work, trying to drown out the ache that clung to him like a shadow. Conversations with friends became mechanical; laughter felt foreign on his lips. The places they had visited together echoed with memories, each one a sharp reminder of what he had lost. He built walls around his heart, determined never to let it shatter that way again.

This melancholy also stirred a deep nostalgia within him-a longing for the simpler days of their early relationship, when laughter filled their home and their worries seemed trivial and distant. He remembered the joyous trips they took to little bed-and-breakfasts by the sea, where they dreamed aloud about the future and made promises under the vast, starry sky. These memories, once sources of comfort, now seemed like scenes from another life, making his heart ache with the desire to reclaim that lost happiness.

As he grappled with these feelings, Arjun also faced the challenge of confronting his own vulnerabilities. He struggled to communicate his fears and desires to anyone, fearing that his words would only hurt. This internal battle not only deepened his sorrow but also made him question his own identity and the very essence of the love he shared with Rani.

Meeting Maya had been unexpected-a gentle touch to his numbed heart. Her warmth slowly seeped through his defenses, promising a new chapter. Yet, as they grew closer, the scars from his past love remained, a constant reminder of the pain that love could bring. Arjun loved Maya, but part of him held back, haunted by the ghost of his first love, and the devastating knowledge of how deeply love could cut.

This experience haunted him, casting a shadow over his ability to fully commit emotionally to Maya, despite his love for her.

The echoes of his past with Rani often surfaced in moments of vulnerability, causing Arjun to withdraw emotionally when Maya needed him most. This was particularly evident during Maya's high-risk pregnancy, a time when she needed Arjun's support and presence.

Maya was his second chance at love, the woman who helped him rebuild after the pain of his first breakup.

Maya's whirlwind romance with Munish had started as a shared dedication to their careers at the bank, where late nights and complex projects were common. As they tackled challenges together, their mutual respect had blossomed into something deeper. Munish, with his unwavering ambition and sharp intellect, was a beacon of inspiration and romance in the high-pressure environment of corporate finance. Maya and Munish's romance began with the spark of intense conversations over steaming cups of coffee in a cozy corner of their favorite café. The aroma of freshly ground coffee beans became a backdrop to their blossoming relationship, as each meeting deepened their connection. Those early coffee dates turned into ritualistic gatherings where they shared not just their favorite blends but also the intricacies of their lives.

Over lattes and cappuccinos, Munish would talk animatedly about his latest business ideas, leaning in closer across the small table, his eyes alight with passion and entrepreneurial spirit. Maya, enchanted by his ambition, would share her own dreams of making a mark in the world with her art, her sketches sometimes sprawling across the napkins between them. Their conversations would flow from professional ambitions to personal beliefs, weaving a tapestry of shared values and mutual respect.

As their cups emptied and the café's ambient music hummed in the background, their discussions would often segue into plans for the future, sometimes sketched out on café napkins or merely spoken into existence between them. These quiet evenings spent discussing dreams and aspirations not only drew them closer but also laid the foundation for a partnership that was as much about emotional connection as it was about supporting each other's aspirations. With each date, their affection grew, framed by the intimate glow of the café, encapsulating a world where only they existed.

Maya had found herself drawn to Munish's passion not only for his career but for life itself. He had a way of making even mundane moments feel magical, and she cherished the way he would look at her as if she were the only person in the room. They celebrated successes together, and when challenges arose, they supported each other unwaveringly.

However, as Maya climbed the corporate ladder, her visions for the future began to shift. Her ambitions, which once aligned so perfectly with Munish's, started to diverge as new opportunities pulled her in different directions. She realized that the life she envisioned for herself might not leave room for the kind of partnership Munish wanted-one deeply rooted in shared daily experiences and intertwined professional lives.

The realization came with a profound sense of loss. Maya struggled with the decision, knowing that moving forward professionally might mean leaving something precious behind. Their last few meetings were tinged with an unspoken understanding that things were changing. When she finally made the decision to leave the bank for a new opportunity, it felt like a door quietly closing on a chapter of her life that she could never reopen.

Letting go of Munish was not just leaving a lover but also leaving a version of herself that could no longer exist. She carried the pain of that loss quietly, a silent ache of what might have been. As she moved on, her heart held a cautious hope, but also a protective wariness, shaped by the knowledge of how deeply paths could fork, leaving old dreams behind in pursuit of new horizons.

Years later, she and Arjun married, and despite his baggage, Maya felt she'd made the right choice. After years of trying, she finally became pregnant, and Arjun seemed like the perfect husband, tending to her needs and showing his love. But with Maya's high-risk pregnancy taking a toll on her health, Arjun found himself yearning for the thrill of romance that his marriage now lacked. Just as he had moved on with Maya after his heartbreak with Rani, he found himself drawn to a new woman: Surbhi, a beautiful and vivacious colleague who reignited a spark he thought he'd lost. What began as casual flirtation soon turned to intimacy, with Arjun finding solace in Surbhi's arms while Maya struggled through her difficult pregnancy.

Unknown to Arjun, Surbhi had her own hidden life. She was in a complex, on-and off relationship with Rakesh, a possessive man who had never truly let go of her. Rakesh, suspicious of Surbhi's fidelity, had begun stalking her, keeping a close eye on her every move. The night Maya was rushed to the hospital to give birth, Arjun and Surbhi met at Maya's house, seeking the privacy they could not find elsewhere. Rakesh, lurking in the shadows, captured it all on film-the embrace, the lingering looks, and the stolen intimacy in a home that wasn't Arjun's alone.

The night that should have been the happiest of Maya's life turned lonely when Arjun chose to leave her side. Hours later, after her daughter Anaya's birth, Maya clung to the hope that he had a valid reason for his absence. But his coldness in the following days and his seeming disinterest in her told her otherwise.

Maya: "You were supposed to be my partner, Arjun. How could you betray me?" Arjun: "It was a mistake, Maya. I don't know how I let it happen."

Then, she received an anonymous message from an unfamiliar number. Attached was a video clip, capturing Arjun and Surbhi together on the night of her labor. As Maya watched, her heartbreak turned to a fierce, steely resolve.

What she didn't share with Arjun-or anyone-was that she had never truly forgotten Munish. After seeing the video, Maya reconnected with him. Old flames rekindled, and the passion they had once shared now provided Maya with solace and strength. Munish, understanding her pain, became her confidant and eventually, her lover once more. Together, they shared laughter, late-night conversations, and the emotional support Maya had missed in her marriage.

Six years passed in silence, as Maya kept her secret affair with Munish and raised her daughter, waiting for the right moment to confront Arjun with the betrayal he thought he'd hidden so well. Then came the twist of fate that provided her with an opportunity for retribution. When Arjun's father passed, he left a large inheritance for Anaya, with the condition that she would inherit it fully at age six.

One evening, when the storm clouds rolled over the mountains, Maya sat Arjun down and told him her own fabricated story of infidelity. She revealed that Anaya was not his biological daughter, hinting that she had been with another man, rekindling her affair with Munish. Arjun was devastated, grappling with the idea that Anaya, the child he adored, was not his own, and that his father's legacy was set to go to a child he believed was born of betrayal.

Faced with the dual revelations of their respective affairs, Maya and Arjun were forced to confront the realities of their relationship, the unresolved issues from their pasts, and the choices that had led them to this juncture. This confrontation became a pivotal moment for both, a chance to address the wounds they had both inflicted and suffered, and to decide whether their love and their shared history were strong enough to forge a path forward, embracing the possibility of healing and a second chance together.

Maya: (crying) "Seeing you with her, it broke me." Arjun: "I would do anything to undo that moment."

In the aftermath, Maya's confession about Anaya being Arjun's daughter shook him to his core. The mix of emotions was overwhelming-betrayal from her deceit, yet a profound joy at discovering this deeper connection to his daughter. As he looked at Anaya, every smile, every innocent question she had ever asked him, took on new, significant meaning. He felt a sudden clarity, a sense of purpose that redefined what he thought was possible for their future.

Maya: "Can we try to forgive each other? For us? For Anaya?" Arjun: "Yes, we owe it to her to try."

Arjun: "Let's start anew, Maya. Truly, from the heart." Maya: "It will take time, Arjun. A lot of time."

Arjun: "I want to rebuild our trust, Maya. Whatever it takes." Maya: "We'll need help. Maybe counseling?" Arjun: "Whatever it takes. I'm in."

With their deep-seated love as a foundation, Arjun and Maya began the painstaking process of rebuilding their trust. The revelation about Anaya acted as a catalyst for them to explore the fractures in their relationship not just with bitterness, but with the intent to heal and grow stronger together. They started attending counseling sessions, where they learned to communicate their fears, insecurities, and hopes more openly. Each session, while challenging, slowly stitched back the seams of their relationship that had come undone.

The commitment to their daughter Anaya became the strongest motivator. They both loved her unconditionally and knew that her happiness depended on their ability to coexist and cooperate lovingly. Weekends were spent together, from picnics in the park to little adventures around the city, which not only brought joy to Anaya but also helped Arjun and Maya rediscover the friendship and affection that had first drawn them together.

As they mended their ties, Arjun's heart gradually opened up again. He found himself forgiving Maya, understanding her actions as those of someone hurt and lost, lashing out in pain rather than malice. Maya, in turn, deeply regretted her deception, and her efforts to make amends were genuine and tireless. She supported Arjun's bonding with Anaya, facilitating moments of connection, celebrating their similarities and gently guiding their understanding of each other.

Through their journey, the couple learned the power of vulnerability and the strength that comes from facing the truth together. Their relationship, once marred by past wounds and secrets, began to blossom anew, characterized by a more profound respect and a steadfast commitment to nurture not only Anaya's life but also the love that had survived the toughest of trials. Together, they forged a new path, one marked by a deep understanding that love, when truly rooted, can endure and adapt beyond life's unpredictable twists.

Simultaneously, they made a pact to renew their commitment to their family. They started by creating new family traditions and spending more quality time together, which included family vacations and weekly outings, allowing them to create new, joyful memories. These activities not only brought fun and lightness back into their lives but also reinforced their bond as a family.

As Arjun and Maya worked on rebuilding their marriage, their efforts were punctuated by moments that rekindled their love and brought them closer than ever.

One evening, they found themselves alone after Anaya's bedtime, seated on their balcony wrapped in a blanket to ward off the chill of the night. The city lights flickered in the distance as Maya broke the silence.

"Remember our first date?" she asked softly, a nostalgic smile playing on her lips.

Arjun turned to her, his eyes reflecting the city's glow. "How could I forget? You wore that green dress and laughed at all my terrible jokes."

Maya chuckled. "I was nervous. You had this way of looking at me, like I was the only one in the room. I missed that."

Arjun reached for her hand, squeezing it gently. "I missed us, Maya. I'm sorry for the walls I put up. I never stopped loving you, but I was scared to let you see how broken I felt."

Maya leaned her head on his shoulder. "I'm sorry too. For everything. I was hurt, and I lashed out instead of facing my pain. I never wanted to hurt you or Anaya."

Their conversation drifted into the night, weaving through apologies and laughter, reconnecting threads long frayed.

A week later, they decided to recreate their first date. As they walked into the same little Italian restaurant, nervous energy tinged with excitement filled the air. They were seated at a cozy corner table, secluded and intimate.

"Arjun, I want to make new memories with you, better ones," Maya said, her eyes earnest.

"I want that too, Maya. Let's start tonight," Arjun replied, his voice filled with hope.

Dinner was a dance of playful banter and shared dishes, each course a step closer together. After dinner, as they walked hand in hand under the starlit sky, Arjun stopped and pulled Maya close.

"Maya, these past weeks, seeing you work so hard for our family, for me... it's reminded me of why I fell in love with you."

Tears welled up in Maya's eyes as she reached up to touch his face. "And you, being here, opening up again-it's everything to me, Arjun."

He leaned down, capturing her lips in a kiss that spoke of promises renewed and futures hopeful. The kiss deepened, their hearts beating in tandem, a silent vow to never let go again.

Through such romantic entanglements, they rekindled the passion and trust that were the foundation of their marriage. Each day brought its own challenges, but facing them together made all the difference, turning past wounds into scars that spoke of survival and a love that endured.

As they celebrated Anaya's sixth birthday, Maya and Arjun looked at each other with a profound appreciation for the journey they had traveled together. They were not only surviving but thriving, proving that their love, fortified by genuine efforts to understand and support one another, was resilient enough to transcend the trials they had faced.

The story of Maya and Arjun concludes with a hopeful note on the power of love and redemption, highlighting that even in the face of profound challenges, a second chance can lead to a stronger, more enduring bond.

Gratitude

THANKYOU FOR READING